J. BERRY

Candid Conundrum

Mysteries in Every Polaroid

JAMAR BERRY

LONDON BY DESIGN PUBLISHING HOUSE LTD.

2022

COPYRIGHT

The events and conversations in this book have been set down to the best of the author's ability, although some names and details have been changed to protect the privacy of individuals.

Every effort has been made to trace or contact all copyright holders. The publishers will be pleased to make good any omissions or rectify any mistakes brought to their attention at the earliest opportunity.

Any resemblance to persons living or dead should be plainly apparent to them and those who know them, especially if the author has been kind enough to have provided their real names and, in some cases, their phone numbers. All events described herein actually happened, though on occasion the author has taken certain, very small, liberties with chronology, because that is his right as an Englishmen.

Author copyright © 2022 by Jamar Z Berry

Publication © 2022 by London By Design Publishing House Ltd.
Contact Details:
LondonByDesignPublishing@gmail.com

ISBN: 978-1-0690286-5-5

Dive headfirst into an exhilarating whirlwind with "Candid Conundrums" - a spellbinding blend of whimsy, mystery, and heart-pounding thrills, sure to keep you on the edge of your seat!

In the heart of a dreamy, bustling city, meet Ruby Berry – a whimsical photographer with a flair for capturing life's most candid moments on her trusty Polaroid camera. Ruby delights in preserving magical snippets of everyday life, whether it's a hearty laugh between friends at a cozy café, an impromptu dance at a bustling train station, or a gentle smile in a sun-dappled restaurant. Her passion? Sharing these joyful snapshots with strangers, leaving them to discover the enchanted glimpses of life she captures.

But when this light-hearted hobby takes a dramatic turn, Ruby finds herself thrust into the heart of a decade-old cold case. The charming snapshots that once brought simple happiness now become critical clues in a high-stakes investigation. Ruby, with her fair skin kissed by freckles, curly ginger hair, and sparkling eyes framed by vibrant glasses, must use her unique talent for capturing the essence of life to unravel a dark and intricate mystery.

Joining Ruby on this heart-racing adventure are her best friends, twin sisters Isabella (Bella) and Olivia (Liv) DuBois. With their raven-black hair, thick eyebrows, mesmerizing eyes, and plump lips, the twins bring a captivating and enigmatic aura to the trio. But it's Ruby's unique charm and infectious spirit that anchor this dynamic threesome, creating a balanced and unshakeable bond.

Together, Ruby, Bella, and Liv embark on a thrilling journey brimming with clues, secrets, and unexpected twists. As they delve deeper into the case, they discover that each photo holds not just a moment in time but a piece of a larger puzzle – one that could change their lives forever.

Get ready for a joyride of mystery and merriment in "Candid Conundrums" – a story where every photo hides a thrilling tale and every moment is a clue waiting to be uncovered. Buckle up and join the adventure where whimsy meets intrigue, and where friendship and courage lead the way to the truth.

Table of Contents

CHAPTER I

The Enchanting Photographer

The soft hum of a bustling city enveloped Ruby Berry as she navigated the vibrant streets, her trusty Polaroid camera swinging gently at her side. The world around her was a kaleidoscope of colors, sounds, and smells, all blending into a symphony that resonated deep within her whimsical spirit. It was a Tuesday morning, but for Ruby, every day had the potential for magic. Her heart danced to the rhythm of the life unfolding around her, and her mind brimmed with possibilities as she searched for her next candid moment.

Ruby was not just any photographer; she was a conjurer of joy, capturing fleeting instances that might otherwise go unnoticed. With her fair skin adorned by playful freckles and curly ginger hair bouncing with every step, she eagerly scanned the faces around her. Each grin, every shared laugh, and those unexpected glances held stories begging to be told. Wearing bright floral overalls layered over a soft white tee and her favorite scuffed sneakers, Ruby exuded an effortless charm that drew people to her.

She reached the lively café at the corner of Maple and 5th, where the scents of freshly brewed coffee mingled with the sweet aroma of pastries wafting through the open windows. It was her go-to spot, a small, cozy nook filled with mismatched furniture and colorful art adorning the walls, each piece bringing its own history. Ruby loved it especially for the patrons who frequented it, each one a potential character in her ongoing tale of whims and wonders.

As she settled into her favorite corner table by the window, Ruby pulled out her Polaroid camera, a vintage beauty with a slightly battered exterior but a spirit as vibrant as the artist who wielded it. Today, she felt an electric tingle of anticipation, as if the universe was whispering secrets meant only for her. This was her sacred ritual – capturing life in its most spontaneous form, then leaving the prints for unsuspecting strangers to find.

Once an innocent pastime, Ruby's hobby had evolved into a delicious obsession, feeding her soul while allowing her an unfiltered lens into the lives of others. With her camera poised and ready, she focused on a group of friends at the next table, their laughter bubbling over like the frothy cappuccinos before them. With a smile stretching from ear to ear, Ruby squeezed the shutter button, and her camera whirred to life, spitting out a developing photograph. As the image materialized, she felt a sense of accomplishment, as if she'd made a piece of happiness immortal.

A few moments later, Ruby gingerly picked up the freshly printed snapshot — a vibrant explosion of joy, capturing the friends mid-laugh, the sunlight filtering through the window and casting a golden glow on their faces. With a glimmer of mischief in her eyes, she made her way to the table, balancing the photo in her hands. "Excuse me," she said, her voice bubbling with enthusiasm, "but would you like to have a little surprise?"

The friends paused, their laughter quieting as they regarded her curiously. "What kind of surprise?" asked a tall girl with curly hair grazing her shoulders.

Ruby grinned. "This!" She held out the photo, the image perfectly encapsulating their infectious joy. "It's yours to keep. Just a little reminder of this beautiful moment."

"Wow, that's incredible!" exclaimed another friend, his eyes widening in surprise.

"Thank you!" the curly-haired girl said, accepting the photo with a look of pure delight. "This is such a lovely idea!"

Ruby beamed, her heart swelling at their reaction. "I believe we all deserve a bit of sunshine in our lives, don't you?" With that, she turned on her heel and made her way back to her corner, her spirit soaring higher than before.

After a few additional snapshots of snippets of happiness — an elderly couple sharing a dessert, a child's awe as they watched the barista create foam art — Ruby felt the familiar pull of inspiration and something deeper bubbling below the surface. The impulse to spread joy was more than just her passion; it was her purpose.

Hours slipped away seamlessly as Ruby continued her routine, taking photographs and spreading smiles, but the chatter in the café slowly softened. As the sun began to dip in the sky, painting it a warm hue of orange and pink, Ruby grabbed her camera and decided it was time to explore the streets beyond the café.

Once outside, the fresh air filled her lungs, invigorating her senses. Ruby wandered down cobblestone streets lined with quaint shops, their windows adorned with artful displays, each telling its own story. A gust of wind tousled her curls, but she welcomed it; it felt like a gentle nudge from the universe, urging her to keep exploring. As she strolled, her eyes were drawn to a glimmering object partially hidden within a flowerbed. Curious, she bent down and discovered a delicate silver locket, intricate in design but tarnished by time.

Picking it up, Ruby examined it, a spark igniting within her. "Oh, how fascinating!" she mused aloud, holding the locket to the fading light. "What stories do you carry within?" She glanced around for its owner but found no one in sight. Carefully, she slipped it into her bag, promising herself to find a way to return it once she uncovered its history.

Absorbed in her thoughts, Ruby began snapping pictures of the lingering sunset, enchanted by the way the colors danced in the sky. With each click, she felt a connection to the world beyond the lens — a tapestry of lives interwoven with her own. However, beneath the joyous surface, an undercurrent of curiosity about the locket nagged at her mind. Perhaps it held significance, a secret waiting to be uncovered.

With the sun now dipping below the horizon, Ruby decided it was time to head home. As she made her way back, she thought about how she could investigate the locket's origins. A thrill raced through her; this could be another adventure, another story waiting to be captured. Perhaps it could even lead to a series of candid shots — people with stories about lost treasures, forgotten memories, and the bonds that tether them to their past.

Upon arriving at her small apartment filled with light and color — walls splashed with her own photographs depicting the beauty of urban life — Ruby felt a mix of excitement and peace wash over her. She dropped her bag on the kitchen table and took a moment to breathe in the familiar scents of her home, where fresh flowers and a hint of paint created a vibrant atmosphere.

After setting down her Polaroid, she pulled the locket from her bag, its coolness contrasting with the warmth of her hand. She turned it over and noticed a small engraving on the back: "Forever Yours, E." The sentiment struck a chord deep within her, sparking her imagination. Who was E? What stories lay behind this delicate piece of jewelry? More importantly, was someone out there still missing it?

Fueled by inspiration, Ruby reached for her laptop and started researching ways to find lost items in the community. A plethora of websites and social media groups popped up, each dedicated to helping reunite lost treasures with their owners. She wondered if she could craft a story around the locket — perhaps a tale of lost love or cherished memories — and use it as a catalyst for her next project. With butterflies in her stomach and a newfound sense of purpose, Ruby spent the evening crafting a plan for her investigation.

She made notes and sketches, carefully mapping out how she would document her journey to uncover the locket's history. Each entry in her notebook transformed into an idea, swirling in a beautiful mess of colors, images, and half-formed dreams. Before she realized it, the moon had risen high in the night sky, casting a silvery glow that seeped through her window and illuminated her workspace. The prospect of her next adventure filled her with energy.

As Ruby blew out the single candle adorning her table — a flickering flame that mirrored the essence of inspiration dancing within her — she felt a renewed sense of connection to the world around her. Her heart raced as she envisioned the stories yet to unfold, the lives she would touch, and the candid moments she would forever preserve.

In that moment, gazing at her collection of photographs lining the walls, she knew she was destined to capture more than just images; she was meant to capture the very essence of life — messy, beautiful, and always full of surprises. And with each new story, each twist of fate that fate might present, Ruby would weave them together, allowing herself and others to see the world through her whimsical lens.

The night deepened, and Ruby drifted into a peaceful slumber, dreams swirling with vivid snapshots of untold stories, luminous sunsets, and perhaps even the heartwarming reunion of a locket with its owner. She was ready for whatever adventure awaited her, unknowingly preparing for a journey that would not only unravel secrets of the past but also lead to friendships that would shine like the stars in the sky.

Little did Ruby know, this adventure would soon turn the world of her photographs into a thrilling conundrum — blending whimsy with mystery in ways she had never imagined. As sleep enveloped her, the streets outside pulsed with life, the world spinning forward with tales just waiting for her to discover. The next chapter of her extraordinary journey was closer than she realized, and the magic was only just beginning.

CHAPTER 2

A Snapshot Leads to Suspicion

Morning light streamed through Ruby's window, spilling across her bedroom in a cascade of gold and orange hues. She stirred, her eyes fluttering open to the cheerful chirping of birds outside. With a yawn, she swung her legs over the edge of the bed, stretching as she took a moment to relish the delightful remnants of her dreams. The locket lay on her bedside table, glinting as if it had a story of its own to share.

After breakfast — a slice of toast and a generous dollop of jam followed by a steaming cup of her favorite herbal tea — Ruby peeled open her laptop to dive into her project. Her fingers danced across the keyboard as she began drafting a post for the local lost-and-found group online. "Have you lost a treasure?" she began, infusing her personality into the text. It was sprinkled with respect for the memories of the past while inviting strangers to share their stories.

As she crafted this digital outreach, her mind fully absorbed in the imaginative possibilities, she couldn't shake the feeling of anticipation that enveloped her. Each click of the keyboard brought forth thoughts of the adventures lying ahead. Yet while she was eager to inspire connections through the locket, another part of her sparked with curiosity about the looser threads of her latest candid photography endeavor.

Remembering the revelations of the previous day, Ruby replayed the images she had captured at the café. Her sessions alight with joy seemed to always hold a dollop of serendipity, and yesterday was no different. As she scanned over the photos again, one particular shot stood out — a snapshot of the friends laughing, framed by the sun. But among the cheerful scene, something unusual nagged her attention.

There it was, an indistinct shadow lurking in the background, partially obscured by a passing patron. Ruby squinted at her computer screen, bringing up the photo in question. The shadow — an ominous, ghostlike presence — danced on the edge of the frame, fleeting, but clear enough to evoke her innate instinct as a storyteller. She could almost hear a whisper woven into the air. What belonged to that figure? Did it belong at all?

Intrigue ignited her imagination; this was familiar territory, a lighthearted investigation ready to unfurl. Ruby knew she couldn't ignore this small curiosity, especially when a slight part of her desired to chase the unexpected mystery that drooped behind her photograph. With her heart racing, she grabbed her Polaroid, rapidly composed, and decided today's mission was to uncover the truth behind the shadow.

She quickly texted Bella and Liv, her spirited twin friends, inviting them to join her for the day. The message read: "Join me for an adventure! I've found something interesting at the café that needs our attention. Let's discover the mystery!"

Less than thirty minutes later, Bella's entrance sent a flurry of fresh energy throughout Ruby's apartment. Her dark raven hair, cascading down in waves, framed her face beautifully. Liv followed behind, her plump lips stretched in a teasing smile as she entered. The duo exuded a magnetic aura that had always complemented Ruby's vibrant nature. Grand gestures weren't necessary between them; their bond was deep-rooted, echoing with laughter and understanding.

"Good morning, sunshine!" Bella exclaimed as she flopped onto Ruby's couch. "What's this mystery you've stirred up?"

"It's sensational!" Ruby replied, a light in her sparkling eyes. "You won't believe what I found in one of my photos. A shadow flickering at the edge of laughter." She excitedly set her laptop on the coffee table, showcasing the image.

Liv leaned closer, her brow furrowed with curiosity. "It looks like you caught something in your candids. What do you think it is?"

"I have no idea," Ruby admitted, biting her lip with growing excitement. "But that's exactly what I plan to find out! I want to revisit the café and see if anyone else recognizes this figure."

"Count us in!" Bella declared, determination blaring from her every word. "What's the plan?"

"First, I want to chat with some of the café patrons who were there yesterday," Ruby explained as she rummaged through her bag, pulling out several prints she had prepared to leave behind as surprises. "And if we can identify the shadowy figure, that's even better. We'll spark more conversations, maybe people will have clues or stories related to it."

"Exciting!" Liv said, her mesmerizing gaze sparkling with enthusiasm. The twins shared a glance, both fueled by Ruby's contagious energy.

They gathered their belongings and set out into the bustling streets. The sun shone brightly above, and Ruby felt invigorated as she led her friends toward the café, visions of possibilities painting her mind.

Upon arriving, she felt an electrifying buzz in the air, a familiar pulse that resonated within her. The café suggested an oracle-like presence — it breathed warmth and comfort into the lives of the people who shared fleeting moments there. As they stepped inside, the comforting aroma of coffee wrapped around them like a warm embrace.

Ruby set up her camera and took a quick portrait of the café, the snapshots containing traces of laughter and love woven within the vibrant walls. The trio wandered through the lively space, surveying familiar faces and scanning for that mystical figure frozen in time.

Finally, Ruby spotted the group that had entertained her eye a day prior. They were grinning and reminiscing at a central table, their laughter intertwining with the café's ambient noise. Summoning her courage, she approached them. Bella and Liv stood by her side, ready to support their friend.

"Hey there! You may not remember me, but I was here yesterday capturing candid moments." Ruby flashed a bright smile. "I took a snapshot of you and your friends, and I have something to ask. Do you mind if I show you a photo?"

The friends looked up, their laughter fading into curiosity. "Sure! What's up?" the curly-haired girl chimed, leaning forward.

With a sense of excitement bubbling in her chest, Ruby presented the photo, her heart racing as she pointed to the shadow in the background. "In this picture, there's a figure behind you all. I'm trying to figure out who it might be," she explained, leaning closer.

The friends exchanged puzzled glances, their excitement waning as they squinted at the picture. "Wow, I didn't notice that before!" said the tallest boy, scratching his head. "That's strange. I don't remember anyone standing behind us."

"What does it look like to you?" Bella prompted, leaning into the conversation.

"Maybe just some random person passing by?" the curly-haired girl suggested, uncertainty creeping into her voice. "But it's weird that they're only in your picture."

Ruby nodded, the group's lack of recognition only feeding the growing curiosity within her. "Can you recall anything unusual that happened during your time here?" she encouraged.

"Not really," Liv chimed in, scanning the room. "But you should actually ask the barista! She's been here forever and knows most of the regular customers."

Ruby felt her heart race. "Right! Let's go talk to her," she agreed, adrenaline flooding her veins.

After a few minutes of casual browsing, they maneuvered over toward the counter where the barista, a woman named Eva with vibrant blue hair scraped back into a bun, was preparing a latte. Noticing Ruby and her friends approaching, Eva flashed them a friendly smile.

"Hey there! Back for some more good vibes?" she asked cheerfully.

"Actually, we were hoping to get some insight from you," Ruby replied, her voice animated with excitement. "I took a candid photo here yesterday, and there's something odd in it — a shadow of a person in the background. Do you happen to remember anything unusual or anyone that might have been here at that time?"

Eva furrowed her brow, leaning closer to glance at the image Ruby was holding. As her eyes widened, a spark of recognition danced across her features. "Wait a minute," she hesitated, glancing around the café as if to confirm something. "I do remember a guy who was sitting alone yesterday, just by the window. He seemed a bit... off. I can't quite put my finger on it."

"What do you mean by 'off'?" Liv pressed, her interest piqued.

Eva paused, choosing her words carefully. "He kept looking around, like he was watching everyone. It was a bit unsettling. I thought maybe he was just waiting for someone, but he never met anyone."

Ruby's curiosity intensified, her mind racing. "Do you know what he looked like?" she asked, leaning in closer to catch every detail.

"Dark clothes, hoodie pulled up, kind of hidden in the shadows. That's why I didn't think much about it at the time. It was just a regular day, you know?"

Ruby's heart thumped louder with each piece of information that poured from Eva. "Any idea about how he left? Did he stick around long?"

"Not sure," she said, shaking her head. "I was busy getting orders out, but when I looked, he was gone. Could have slipped out without anyone noticing."

A chill ran down Ruby's spine. The shadow in her photograph was becoming more potent, taking shape in her mind as something tangible, almost sinister. "Thanks for sharing that!" Ruby responded, excitement blending with a sense of urgency. "We're going to dig deeper into this."

After thanking Eva, the trio huddled together in a booth, jubilant but cautious. "So we have a lead now," Ruby said, her eyes sparkling with determination. "It's time to piece together this mystery."

"But what's our next move?" Liv asked, bouncing her knee anxiously.

"I think we need to see if anyone else remembers this man," Ruby responded, resolutely. "Plus, I want to revisit the spot he was sitting in to capture more hints."

Bell, always the strategist, leaned back with her arms crossed. "What if we create a bit of buzz about it? We could share the photo on social media, and see if anyone recognizes him?"

Ruby nodded eagerly. "Yes! If we send it out into the world, maybe someone will recognize the figure. There might even be locals who noticed him yesterday."

"Let's do it!" Liv exclaimed, enthusiasm blending with adventure. The trio felt united in this impulsive investigation, emboldened by the mystery that lay ahead.

They gathered their things, the vibration of exhilaration pulsing through them as they stepped back onto the busy streets, ready to chase shadows together. Ruby's heart raced with anticipation, knowing they were now drawn into a story far more intricate than she'd ever anticipated. It was no longer just about capturing candid moments but uncovering the threads of a mystery — an adventure that fundamentally promised to intertwine their fates with that of a total stranger.

As they roamed through the city, the shadows lengthened, hinting at the stories hiding just beneath the surface. Ruby felt the weight of something significant brewing on the horizon, drawing them closer to a tapestry of lives waiting to be intersected. Little did they know, the shadow that started in a mere photograph would lead them far beyond their cozy café and into a web of intrigue that bound them to secrets begging to be revealed.

CHAPTER 3

The Twins Join the Fun

The thrill of uncovering a mystery invigorated Ruby as she walked alongside Bella and Liv through the bustling streets of their beloved city. With each step, the lingering excitement of the café adventure swirled within her, an intoxicating mix of curiosity and anticipation. The trio shared purposeful glances – their unspoken agreement to dive headfirst into the unknown was stronger than ever.

After mapping out their plan, they decided to take a detour before returning to their favorite hangouts. As they strolled past the eclectic shops that lined Maple Street, whimsical signs and brightly painted storefronts beckoned them in. Ruby could feel the energy flowing around her, as if the city itself were alive, ready to offer pieces of inspiration for their detective work.

"Let's check out that vintage shop!" Bella pointed enthusiastically at a quaint storefront adorned with colorful paper lanterns and a window filled with delightful odds and ends. It was a treasure trove of curiosities that Ruby and her friends often explored together. The allure of the shop seemed to melt their worries and fuel their playful spirits.

"Great idea! We might find something that's a clue for our investigation," Ruby chirped, her eyes sparkling with excitement.

Inside, the scent of aging wood and old books enveloped them like a warm hug. The store was a labyrinth of trinkets, vintage clothing, and framed artwork, every inch a potential story waiting to be told. Ruby loved how time seemed to stand still in places like this, allowing her imagination to run wild among treasures that had their own histories.

Bella immediately darted toward a rack filled with colorful dresses, her discerning eye valuing the beauty of each piece. "Look at this!" she exclaimed, holding up a flowy sundress with a bohemian print. "I'm telling you, this will look great at the gallery show!"

Liv perused a shelf full of curios – small figurines and old clocks that ticked with character. "And this," she said, picking up a delicate porcelain cat that looked oddly regal, "is perfect for your collection, Ruby!"

While her friends explored, Ruby wandered deeper into the shop, her heart racing with a sense of adventure. She loved the way they could become side characters in a fantasy world whenever they stepped inside.

As she wandered through the aisles, she cocooned herself in reveries, pondering the shadowy figure from her photographs. Thoughts of who he might be and what story he carried flooded her mind. This unexpected mystery had bound Ruby, Bella, and Liv tightly together, fueling their shared passion for unearthing secrets.

Then, out of the corner of her eye, something glinted from a dusty shelf that stood to one side. Pulling it into focus, Ruby could see it was an old, tarnished camera — vintage in style and seemingly forgotten. Fascinated, she approached to examine it more closely. The camera had a faded brown leather casing, and a tangle of frayed cords hung from it like vines, begging for attention.

"Hey, check this out!" Ruby called, calling her friends over. Bella and Liv soon appeared, peering curiously at the camera.

"What an antique!" Bella exclaimed, reaching out to touch the delicate device. "If only it could tell its story."

Ruby picked it up, feeling the weight of its history in her hands. "What if this camera belonged to someone who captured moments just like I do? Maybe it holds unspent memories and creates magic."

Liv's eyes lit up. "What if we could restore it somehow? It might just inspire you further in your investigation!"

"That's a great idea!" Ruby said, her excitement peaking. "But more importantly, I wonder if it even works. Imagine what stories it could tell if we could develop some photographs!"

Engulfed in thoughts of the possibilities, Ruby approached the shopkeeper — a bespectacled elderly man with kind eyes, engrossed in a worn-out book by the counter. "Excuse me, sir?" she asked politely. "How much is this camera?"

The man peeked up from his book, his eyes sparkling with intrigue. "Ah, the old Cooper case! You have a good eye, young lady," he said. "That camera has been sitting here for years, waiting for someone passionate like you to notice it. For you? I'd say fifteen dollars."

"Fifteen? Really?" Ruby gasped, glancing at her friends. "That's a steal! Can we get it, please?"

"Of course!" Bella replied, pulling out her wallet. "Consider it a way to celebrate this mysterious adventure we're on."

With the camera now in hand, Ruby felt yet another thrill of excitement. She couldn't wait to dive into its potential story.

They left the vintage shop, sunlight flooding their path and fueling their spirits anew. The camera felt like a charm, adding more mystery to their already brewing adventure. With newfound determination, they made their way back to the café, ready to embark on their detective work.

Once they arrived, they settled into a cozy booth near the same table where they had first noticed the shadowy figure. Ruby pulled out her Polaroid again, instinctively wanting to reacquaint herself with the environment that held so many unanswered questions. With the café bustling with chatter and laughter, she began clicking away, capturing the essence of everyday life around her — capturing soul and stories waiting to be discovered.

"Okay, team," Ruby began, her fingers fired up from her quick shoot. "Let's go through our plan. First, we share the photo on social media to fish for anyone who has seen the figure. Then, we can start asking questions from people sitting around this cafe today. Local residents may have seen something or someone that didn't seem quite right."

Liv nodded, scribbling notes on a napkin, her ever-organized nature shining through. "Let's also collect information from the regulars we see here. They might have noticed the man, and we can track down when he arrived and left yesterday."

Bella's eyes glinted with mischief. "Plus, we have that gorgeous camera we just bought! We can create a fun little experiment with it. What if we take pictures of customers now and see if anyone from this afternoon recognizes their own snapshots?"

After a moments pause, Ruby beamed at the enthusiasm radiating from her friends. "That's brilliant! Imagine if this mystery intertwines with our photos. Not only do we find clues, but we create stories, too."

They quickly set up to take their photos — a mix of silliness and determination. Bella drew people in effortlessly, her charm inviting others to pose with her, while Liv captured the prominent moments of joy through her sharp-lensed focus.

As the camera captured smiles, Ruby felt her heart swell with pride. With each new snapshot, the excitement vibrated between them, manifesting into a tangible thread that drew them closer to the answers they sought.

After a whirlwind of snapping photos and engaging with patrons, the trio sat together once again, blissful smiles adorning their faces. Ruby set her camera on the table and leaned in closer, her eyes sparkling.

"Let's show the world this little mystery we've pulled ourselves into," she said as she pulled out her phone, ready to post the enigmatic photo of the shadowy figure.

As they prepared to share their discoveries on social media, a tall figure caught Ruby's eye across the café. It was the same curious individual whose shadow had started this entire caper. He sat in an unassuming corner, his hood drawn low over his face, the same familiar aura of suspicion about him.

"Guys," Ruby whispered, instinctively inching lower in her seat. "I think that might be him. The guy from the photo!"

Holding her breath, she alerted her friends, and they quietly turned in unison to observe the figure without drawing attention.

"Should we say something?" Liv whispered, her voice barely above a whisper.

"I think we should approach him," Bella suggested, her courage shining. "If he's haunting our memories, we can ask him what he knows!"

Before Ruby could voice her thoughts, Bella was already standing up, her feet carrying her toward the mysterious figure, confidence guiding her every step. A mix of fear and admiration washed over Ruby. She'd always admired Bella's boldness, but the untamed urge to solve the mystery swirled in Ruby's chest.

"Wait!" Ruby called softly, surging forward to follow Bella. "Let's not spook him."

As they approached, the man looked up. Time seemed to freeze for a moment as their eyes met. In that fleeting instance, Ruby felt a jolt of recognition against the tension in the air. He was not only a stranger but someone in search of his own narrative — lost and adrift, like the shadows of their lives.

"Excuse me," Bella began, her voice steady and curious, "but we were hoping to ask about the photograph taken here yesterday. We noticed something interesting with your... uh... shadow."

At the mention of the photograph, the man's brow furrowed as if something deep within was stirred awake. Ruby held her breath, anticipation echoing in her chest.

"Photograph?" he repeated, his voice barely escaping the confines of his hood. "What photograph?"

Ruby's heart raced. This was the moment everything would either blossom into clarity or dissolve into ambiguity. With apprehension, she stepped forward, ready to unveil the previous day's mystery, ready to confront the enigma before them.

"Would you mind sharing what you know?" she asked gently, her voice steady, despite her trembling heart. "We've been trying to figure things out since yesterday."

The man hesitated, the shadows lifting momentarily from his features, revealing piercing green eyes that flashed with a touch of vulnerability. "Maybe I can help you... but it's... complicated."

It was a moment suffused with tension, but Ruby could sense the potential within that hesitation — a tale waiting to unfurl. Bella and Liv held their breaths beside her, sharing the charged atmosphere that lingered like a delicate film stretched between them.

"Then let's talk," Ruby said, emboldened with a sense of unity. "We're all ears."

They took a seat across from him, their hearts blending with the mystery, each of them poised for a new chapter in this unfolding story. And little did they know, the shadowy figure would lead them down a path of revelations, weaving their lives — tangled but intertwined — into the threads of fate, suspense, and unexpected truths.

CHAPTER 4

Digging into the Past

The café buzzed with life as Ruby, Bella, Liv, and their mysterious new acquaintance settled into their vibrant booth. The air was thick with anticipation, and the faint scent of espresso lingered around them, invigorating their spirits as they prepared to unravel the enigma surrounding the shadowy figure from the photograph.

"Honestly, I'm surprised you noticed me at all," the man said, a hint of amusement flashing in his green eyes, which contrasted starkly against his otherwise guarded demeanor. "Most people just glance at the photographs without looking too closely."

"I guess we're interested in the stories behind the faces," Ruby responded, her enthusiasm palpable. "I'm Ruby, by the way. And these are my friends, Bella and Liv."

"Nice to meet you. I'm Jace," he said, leaning back in his seat but remaining cautious. "So, what about that photograph got you curious?"

With her heart steadying, Ruby explained, "I've been taking candid photographs around the city as a way to spread joy and capture the beauty of everyday life. But that photo from yesterday… it has you in the background appearing kind of… well, ominous." She hesitated to introduce too much drama, recalling how jovial the moment was for the friends she had captured.

"Your shadow kind of contrasts with their laughter," Bella added, trying to balance the conversation with humor to ease any tension.

Jace chuckled softly, but it didn't quite reach his eyes. "I didn't mean to impose. I thought I could just blend into the background."

Eager to dig deeper, Ruby pressed on. "Can you tell us what you were doing there? You mentioned it might be complicated."

Jace rubbed the back of his neck, his expression shifting from amusement to something heavier. "I was hoping to catch a glimpse of someone. It's part of... a personal investigation of my own." The weight of his words hung in the air, transforming the atmosphere around them into something weighty and intimate.

"An investigation?" Liv's curiosity intensified. "What kind of investigation? Are you looking for someone?"

Jace glanced around the café as if he were scanning for prying ears. "Essentially, it's about a person who went missing ten years ago. I believe it was someone close to me—a friend who disappeared from this area." He took a deep breath, collecting his thoughts. "After all this time, I've finally decided to piece together the fragments of the past."

Ruby felt a shiver run down her spine, the cool tendrils of fate wrapping around them. "That's... really deep," she said tentatively. "Was this friend connected to the old case everyone around here seems to know about?"

"Yes, exactly," Jace replied, his eyes narrowing as the realization sunk in. "Everyone refers to it as 'the cold case of Maple Street.' It was all over the news for a while but was eventually forgotten. That's why I came back here — to figure out what really happened."

"Tell us more about it!" Bella encouraged, her expression shifting from curiosity to genuine concern. "What do you know?"

Jace leaned in, the edges of his guard softening a little, and Ruby felt an electric charge of intimacy stretching between them. "Her name was Emma. We were childhood friends, and she took those streets every day, passing by that café. One day, she just never came back," he said, shaking his head as if trying to shake off the painful memories. "I've spent years searching, moving from one thread to another, but I've never been able to find solid leads."

Ruby could feel the gravity of Jace's words anchoring her to the moment. "Do you think she might be connected to my photographs? I mean, I captured what could be snippets of time, clues left behind."

Jace searched her face, gauging her sincerity. "If you caught the right moment, with the right clues... there's a slim chance. But what exactly are you proposing?"

"I want to help you find her," Ruby announced, surprising even herself. The words tumbled out, guided by an instinct she couldn't ignore. "This might be exactly the adventure I've been searching for, and it aligns perfectly. You and I can collaborate, investigate the past together, and use my photography to uncover hidden tales."

Bella and Liv exchanged eager glances, sensing the opportunity unfolding before them. "We can be your 'investigative team'!" Bella chimed in. "We'll support you both every step of the way."

Jace's eyebrows furrowed momentarily; surprise flickered across his face. "Are you sure? I don't want you to get dragged into something dangerous."

"Dangerous or not, we've already started on this adventure," Ruby replied, determination hardening her voice. "Besides, it's just as much your story as it is ours now."

"Okay, then," Jace said, a hint of a smile returning as the weight on his chest began to lift. "Where do we start?"

"The photographs!" Ruby exclaimed, her heart racing as she thought of her camera. "If I can capture more candid moments around here, maybe something will resonate with you. Perhaps someone will remember Emma or know a piece of the old case that connects to what I caught on camera."

"And we can also research local records and resources," Liv added, tapping on her phone for notes. "We might be able to find old news reports or archives about Emma's disappearance."

Bella interjected, "We should also talk to the regulars again, especially those who have been around for a long time. They might hold memories you'd never expect."

A sense of purpose radiated within the group, each of them blending their unique talents and energies. Jace began to share details about Emma, painting a vivid picture of her life as they all gathered around the booth. She'd been a free spirit, spirited and adventurous with a penchant for exploring the city's art festivals and open-mic nights. The more they spoke, the more Ruby felt the connection deepen among them.

Once they gathered a wealth of memories and points of reference, it was time to put their plan into action. The trio shifted gears from inspiration to execution, buzzing with anticipation as they stepped into the action outside the café.

"First, let's head back to the old park where Emma used to hang out," Jace suggested, leading the way. "It's just around the corner. She loved the art installations there, often spending hours sketching or people-watching. If she was anywhere, she would have been there."

As they made their way to the park, Ruby felt a swell of excitement mixed with a tinge of nervousness. This was uncharted territory, and with every step, they forged a bond that was grounded in shared determination to uncover the truth.

Arriving at the park, the afternoon sun bathed everything in a golden hue, the leaves shimmering lazily in the mild breeze. Art installations danced in the sunlight, urging Ruby to capture their beauty through her lens.

"Let me take a few shots of this place," she declared, raising her camera as she meandered through the park. "We should encapsulate the spirit Emma loved the most."

As Ruby froze moments in time, Jace shared more stories about Emma's personality, detailing her vivid enthusiasm for life. Bella and Liv played a game of guessing which piece of art was Emma's favorite, their laughter echoing against the vibrant backdrop.

"Emma was so drawn to the unconventional," Jace reminisced with a nostalgic smile. "She used to say art should challenge people's perceptions. One of her favorites was a large, colorful mural just over there." He pointed to a wall adorned in a riot of colors depicting a dreamlike landscape, painted by a local artist years ago.

Continuing to weave pieces of Emma's affection and personality, the group lost track of time. However, with each captured photo and shared memory, Ruby often found herself glancing back at Jace. She could see the weight of grief he carried, but with every shared story, the weight seemed to lighten, allowing glimpses of hope to shine through.

"Let's try talking to people nearby," Liv suggested, recalling Ruby's initial idea. "We might find someone who recognizes the mural or even remembers Emma."

"Right! I'll pull out the social media post," Ruby said, her excitement spiking as she rummaged through her bag, pulling out her phone. "Let's tag the photo of the mural, add something about Emma, and see if anyone replies!"

Bella grabbed the camera, capturing Ruby's initial exuberance as she posted. They watched as the excitement of reaching out to the community bubbled up, the feeling of connection and shared journey arising among them.

"Now, let's group chat with locals," Jace said, scanning the park for potential witnesses. "Watch for anyone who looks like they might have been around this area long enough to know about Emma or the mural."

The sun angles shifted slightly as they approached older park-goers sitting on nearby benches, enjoying the gentle warmth of the afternoon. It seemed promising as Ruby cautiously addressed one of the gentlemen with a friendly smile.

"Excuse me, sir," she began, "we're trying to learn more about someone who used to come to this park a lot—her name was Emma, and we believe she went missing around ten years ago. Do you recall her at all?"

The man furrowed his brow, a thoughtful look crossing his face as he scrutinized Ruby, then Jace. "Emma, you say? My memory isn't what it used to be, but I reckon I remember hearing about that child. A good soul, she was. Terribly sad the way she... disappeared." His eyes glistened as the weight of the past settled into the present.

"She came here frequently?" Ruby prompted gently, hoping to coax more information from him.

"Oh yes, all the time," the man replied, nodding solemnly. "She used to come with her sketchpad, daydreaming up stories or capturing portraits of the life she saw." He gestured towards the mural. "She loved this place, you know? Even created a few pieces herself for the community art show before she... went missing."

"Do you happen to have any more details?" Liv asked, leaning closer, her eyes shining with determination. "Anything at all?"

The man hesitated before continuing. "The last I heard, she went missing after an art opening down by the river. Rumors went around, but no one knows what truly happened. It was like she vanished into thin air."

Ruby silently noted the details, her mind racing with excitement and sorrow. Emma seemed like someone who had a vivid presence, only to be erased from memory. The shadowy figure, the moments captured by her camera — all of it was weaving together into a profound story that demanded to be told.

As they finished the conversation and thanked the man, Ruby's heart felt heavy yet full, a concoction of emotions melding into something raw and potent. With a silent agreement, the four of them returned to their table.

"I have a feeling we're getting closer," Ruby said, her eyes brightening with excitement tinged with genuine emotion. "Each story, each piece of evidence connects us to Emma. I would love to capture this journey, preserve the essence of her story."

"That's what this is," Jace said, his voice steady. "The connection lies between the photographs, the words from the locals, and the passion for finding the truth. This journey isn't just about her anymore; it's about us, too."

Bella and Liv nodded, equally entranced by the prospect of a shared adventure that far exceeded their expectations.

Determined and resolute, the group returned to the café, where they planned to map out the next steps in their investigation. Ruby's camera clicked as she caught snapshots of their afternoon, moments weaving together into a tapestry more vivid than any storybook dream.

As the sun dipped lower in the sky, casting an amber glow throughout the café, they each felt a renewed sense of purpose. They had begun an extraordinary journey that led them all to deeper connections — not only among themselves but to the threads of lives entwined in the tapestry of their city's history.

They were all part of something greater now, embarking on an investigation that would push the boundaries of friendship, uncover hidden truths, and illuminate shadows long forgotten, reuniting them with a lost friend seeking light from the past.

CHAPTER 5

The First Clue

The café brimmed with laughter and the soft clinking of coffee cups as Ruby, Bella, Liv, and Jace gathered around their table the next morning, fueled by coffee and a shared determination. The day was bright, promising a sense of adventure as they dove deeper into the mystery of Emma's disappearance. With their notes spread across the table, ideas and theories intermingled with excitement, flowing like the sunlight streaming through the tall café windows.

"Okay," Ruby began, pulling everyone's attention. "Based on what we discovered yesterday, our first lead seems to be the art opening by the river. If that was the last place Emma was seen, we need to follow that trail." She highlighted the key phrase in her notes, the ink a solid reminder of the importance of the moment.

"I could practically sense the vibrant energy radiating from that event. If she created art for the show, maybe it could lead us to more people who knew her. Perhaps someone remembers her from that night," Bella chimed in, her dark eyes twinkling with excitement.

Jace nodded, his thoughts visibly deepening. "That's potentially our next move. But it was ten years ago. Finding that original artwork might not be straightforward. Records might be sparse."

Liv leaned forward, her fingers tapping rhythmically on the table. "What if we reach out to the local art community? There could be galleries or artists that remember the show, and they might have archived records."

"That's brilliant!" Ruby exclaimed, her enthusiasm sparking like fireworks. "We can visit local galleries today and ask about the event. If Emma showcased artwork there, it might shed light on what happened afterwards."

As they scoured through various local gallery websites, they stumbled upon the name of the gallery that organized the event: "Canvas & River." It was one of the more popular galleries in the area, known for hosting a wide range of community and individual art shows.

"Let's start there," Jace suggested. "If anyone will have memories from that night, it's the people at Canvas & River."

With a plan in place, they finished their coffees and made their way toward the gallery. The street buzzed with weekend energy; artists set up stalls, musicians played lively tunes, and the aroma of street food wafted through the air, saturating their senses with potential stories waiting to be discovered.

Upon arriving, Ruby marveled at the gallery's exterior — an old brick building with large, inviting windows lined with vibrant artwork. Inside, the warmth of wooden floors and the meticulous arrangement of pieces sparked an instant connection. The gallery exuded creativity, beckoning stories like moths to a flame.

As they stepped inside, a friendly receptionist greeted them. "Welcome to Canvas & River! How can I help you?" she asked, her cheerful demeanor instantly making them feel at ease.

"Hi! We're here to inquire about an art opening that took place ten years ago," Ruby said, stepping forward with a hopeful smile. "We're looking for information on a young woman named Emma who showcased her art there."

The receptionist raised an eyebrow, her friendly smile wavering for a moment as she processed Ruby's question. "Oh, that would have been one of our community events. I do remember someone named Emma—it was quite a significant show. However," she hesitated, "it was overshadowed by the unfortunate incident that followed shortly after."

Ruby's heart sank as she saw the shift in the woman's demeanor. "What incident?" she asked, her curiosity piqued but careful not to overwhelm the receptionist.

"There was a disappearance that happened that night," the receptionist explained gently. "Emma was one of the last people seen leaving the gallery. After the event, she never came home."

An icy chill spread through Ruby, but she maintained her composure. "Do you have any information about what happened? Did anyone see anything suspicious?"

The receptionist hesitated again, her brow furrowing as if wrestling with memories she had long buried. "There were some reports, but... it's been years. If you're seeking detailed accounts, you might want to check local police records. Their investigation fell quiet after a while, and many people tried to forget."

Ruby exchanged glances with Bella, Liv, and Jace, their expressions all reflecting a mix of curiosity and determination.

"Do you still have any records or archives from that event?" Liv inquired, sensing the need to dig deeper. "Anything that could provide insight?"

"Let me see what I can find," the receptionist replied, her tone shifting to one of professional hospitality. She motioned for them to take a seat as she retreated into the back office.

As they sat anxiously awaiting her return, Ruby pulled out her Polaroid camera, feeling the urge to capture the bustling atmosphere around them. She took a quick snapshot of Jace, who absentmindedly pressed a finger against his chin, deep in thought.

"Do you think this could lead us to something tangible?" Jace mused, watching Liv fidget with her notebook as if brainstorming ideas.

"It has to," Ruby replied, determination lacing her voice. "We need to connect with the people who might have been there when it happened. There has to be someone out there who remembers something."

Moments later, the receptionist reappeared, carrying a stack of old papers. "I managed to gather some old documents regarding the event," she said, placing them onto the table with an air of careful reverence. "But beyond that, I recommend you check local news archives as well. They should have covered the incident closely."

Ruby flipped through the documents, her pulse quickening as she absorbed the faded information while scanning for any mention of Emma's artwork or eyewitness accounts from that fateful evening.

"Here it is!" she exclaimed suddenly, causing her friends to lean in closer. "Look at this—it says Emma had created a piece called 'Whispers of the River.' It was featured prominently, and several people commented on how moving it was. We should find out what happened to that piece."

"What else does it say?" Bella's curiosity continued to rise as they dug deeper into the intriguing documentation.

"It says it was a combination of multimedia installation — paints, textures, all inspired by the river itself," Ruby read aloud, her pulse racing. "She invited viewers to delve into their personal stories. Some said it was hauntingly beautiful; it has a hint of melancholy, contrasting its vibrancy."

"How fascinating," Jace said, his interest visibly piqued. "If she was channeling her emotions into her art like that, it might explain why she connected so deeply with her past — or possibly the shadows that followed her."

Ruby nodded in agreement. "Let's see if we can track down that artwork or at least discover who might know about its whereabouts now. If it still exists, it might be our best clue yet."

The receptionist returned with a newspaper clipping from the week after the art opening and laid it on the table. "This article might also give you leads; it mentions witnesses from that night."

"Thank you so much!" Ruby exclaimed, feeling a rush of gratitude wash over her. She took a moment to read through the juicy headlines and dramatic accounts of the events that transpired that night, detailing the artists, patrons, and the eeriness that clouded the gallery.

As Ruby perused the details, a familiar chill crawled up her spine, fueled by the weight of the article. The tragic tone and painful testimonials illustrated the hole left in the community's heart.

The receptionist motioned vaguely towards a corner of the gallery. "There may be some archived photographs from the event in that storage area if you're interested. You can see if any of the attendees are captured in them."

"Absolutely!" Ruby said, her heart racing with fervor. "Let's check it out."

The receptionist led them toward a spacious room filled with boxes and organized files, emphasizing how it might take some time to sift through. Ruby, always eager to embrace the challenge, began rummaging excitedly through the stored items, her eyes alight with possibility.

As they rifled through boxes and folders, something shiny caught Ruby's eye. She picked up a framed black-and-white photograph encased in dust and uncertainty, holding it up for her friends to see. The picture portrayed the gallery's interior during the opening, filled with people admiring the art.

"Look!" she exclaimed, her voice barely concealing her excitement. Upon studying the photo closely, Ruby felt a sharp intake of breath. "It's Emma's piece! Right there at the back!" She pointed to the wall where the artwork had been displayed — the very piece, "Whispers of the River," stood prominently amidst the crowd, evoking a palpable emotional connection.

The moment of revelation hung in the air.

Jace leaned closer, studying the photo carefully. "And look," he noted, tracing a finger along the frame. "There is a man with dark clothes and a hood standing off to the side, partially hidden in the crowd. Could that possibly be...?"

The four friends exchanged glances, their hearts racing in unison.

"It's possible," Ruby said breathlessly. "He could have been there that night. This could be a significant clue leading us closer to Emma's story."

"Let me take a quick picture of this," Bella said excitedly, her adoration for the unexpected connections feeding their hopes. Ruby shifted in her seat to accommodate Bella's shot, securing the photograph as a tangible piece of evidence that would aid their investigation.

As the day unfolded before them, filled with newfound energy and determination, Ruby could sense they were on the brink of a major breakthrough. They had begun digging into the past, unearthing threads that waited folding into the present. The path to uncovering Emma's story was becoming ever clearer.

"Let's make a plan to digitize this photograph and post about it online," Ruby stated, clutching the photo with reverence. "We can also ask if anyone recognizes the man in the background. Maybe he's someone who's still around or even a witness."

"Definitely," Liv agreed, her excitement bubbling over. "This could lead us to a critical breakthrough!"

With their spirits soaring, they left the gallery, the bright sunlight illuminating their path. Each heartbeat echoed with urgency as they continued their quest. Ruby knew they were quickly becoming a part of a treasure trove of stories that would interlace with their own.

As they stepped into the bustling streets, the kind of adventure they had always dreamed of unfolded at their feet

— a mystery ignited with emotion, danger, love, and loss, all waiting to be uncovered. Together, they would illuminate the shadows, transforming whispers of the past into tales that would resonate far beyond their imaginations.

CHAPTER 6

The Café Connection

The sun hung high in the sky, bathing the city in warm light as Ruby, Jace, Bella, and Liv made their way back to the café where their journey began. With each step, Ruby felt a fresh surge of determination. Armed with the photograph of Emma's previous exhibition and buzzing from the promise of what they were uncovering, the group crossed the street with a renewed sense of purpose.

"Let's see if we catch some of the regulars today," Liv said as they entered the café, the familiar aroma of freshly brewed coffee wrapping around them like a comforting blanket. "They might remember that terrible night or anything leading up to it."

Ruby nodded, her gaze sweeping over the room as they found a cozy booth at the back. "It's the perfect setting to share Emma's story. We've got this."

They settled into their seat, anticipation mingling with excitement. The café was packed with patrons enjoying their midday break, laughter and chatter swirling around them like a comforting melody. Bella reached for her phone, eager to document everything. "Let's post about the photo and our findings so far on social media. If we can get the word out, we might just stumble upon someone who remembers Emma or that night," she proposed.

Jace leaned forward, draggy fingers tapping with urgency against the table. "This café has been a fixture in her life; people here might have witnessed something pivotal. I feel like we need to spark conversations while waiting for responses online. We can approach people directly."

Ruby felt her pulse quicken. "You're right; it's time to dig deeper into the café connection."

Before they could put their plan into action, Eva, the friendly barista from their previous visit, approached their table with a genuine smile. "Hey there! Back for more candid moments?" she joked, wiping her hands on a towel.

"Actually, we're here on a mission," Ruby replied, unable to contain her excitement. "We're investigating Emma's disappearance, and we'd love to chat with some of the regulars who might have known her."

Eva's expression softened, her eyes flaring with recognition. "Oh, Emma! I remember her well. She was such a brilliant soul. Are you all serious about finding out what happened?"

"Yes," Ruby said earnestly. "We just came from Canvas & River and found out she had an art piece there called 'Whispers of the River.' It was displayed during an art opening the last night she was seen. We're hoping to track down those final moments."

The barista's brow furrowed, and she nodded slowly. "That night is forever etched in my memory. It was just a regular evening until… it wasn't." She lowered her voice as she glanced around the café to ensure they weren't overheard. "I'll let you know, many people have tried to move past it here, but some can't help but remember."

Encouraged by Eva's response, Ruby leaned in closer. "Were you here that night? Did you notice anything unusual?"

Eva hesitated for a moment, as if weighing her words. "I don't want to stir up old wounds, but yes, I was on shift. Emma had that captivating piece of art that drew in the crowd. There were whispers of how she was so passionate about her work. But I distinctly remember a man—dark, hooded—lingering by the entrance. He kept watching her throughout the event."

Ruby's heart raced. "You mean the shadowy figure? Could it have been the same person captured in our photograph?"

"I'm not certain," Eva replied, her eyes clouded with contemplation. "But I remember feeling uneasy. It wasn't just me; other customers picked up on it too. He was there, and then he was gone."

"Did anyone recognize him?" Liv asked, her curiosity rising.

"No one approached him; he usually just sat alone. Most people found it odd but didn't think much of it—until Emma went missing," Eva said with a sigh. "Looking back, it feels haunting. I always wondered what happened to him, as he just vanished after that night."

The air around the booth shifted, a heavy weight settling in. They had been looking for connections, and now another thread unraveled before them, leading them deeper into the mystery.

"What else do you remember?" Jace pressed gently, seeking every detail contained in Eva's memories.

"There was an older gentleman who seemed to keep an eye on Emma as well. He was speaking to her—older, distinguished-looking—until that other guy showed up. It was like he was drawn to her, his focus almost… possessive," Eva recalled, her voice growing softer with each detail shared.

Ruby's heart raced with new questions cascading through her mind. "Could you describe him?"

"I can't recall exactly, but all I remember is that he was polite and engaging—a total gentleman. It seemed like Emma had a connection with him. They shared laughs while the other guy loomed behind."

It was a puzzle piece interwoven into the narrative.

"Do you think he might still come back here?" Bella asked, her eyes alight with hope.

Eva shook her head subtly. "I haven't seen him since. After Emma disappeared, the café became a quiet place for a long while for those of us who knew her."

As the barista turned to attend to other customers, Ruby felt the walls around her close in slightly, thick with the emotion of the past. "I wish we had more leads."

Jace, ever perceptive, gently placed his hand over hers, grounding her. "Remember, we're in this together. Every detail matters, and this is just the beginning. Perhaps we can head over to talk to the other patrons."

"Great idea! We can show the photograph of Emma's art piece and ask about who else might have been in the café that night," Liv suggested, the gears in her mind already turning.

Fuelled by a renewed sense of purpose, Ruby and her friends spread out across the café, approaching various tables. Each engagement was imbued with a mix of hope and uncertainty, each stranger a potential ally in piecing together the mystery.

"Excuse me," Ruby began at one table, where a group of three were enjoying brunch. "We're investigating a missing person's case—do you remember Emma? She frequented this café?"

The group exchanged glances, interest piqued. "Yeah! I remember her," responded a woman with shoulder-length hair, her voice threading with nostalgia. "She was always drawing in her notebook or chatting with her friends. Such a tragic story."

"Did you notice anything unusual that night?" Ruby probed eagerly.

"Not really; I was focused on a presentation I was prepping for," muttered a man alongside. "But I do think I caught sight of someone in a hooded jacket lingering outside."

"Another hooded figure?" Jace said, a flicker of recognition sparking in his eyes. "Do you recall anything more about them?"

"No, sorry. It was just a quick glance through the window," the man replied, shrugging his shoulders. "But I do remember Emma's smile. She had the warmth that attracted people to her."

Encouraged by their memories, Ruby and her friends moved from table to table, unearthing bits of understanding, small fragments of that fateful night. Most patrons remembered Emma fondly but couldn't provide specifics about what might have occurred leading up to her disappearance.

Just as Ruby felt the energy dwindling, they approached a table where an older couple sat quietly enjoying coffee, their faces illuminated by the sunlight streaming through the window.

49

"Excuse us," Bella said softly. "We're looking for information about Emma, a girl who used to frequent this café. Do you remember her?"

Both the man and woman exchanged glances, their expressions shifting from contentment to recognition. "Oh yes, we remember her," the woman said, her voice trembling with emotion. "She was so full of life and promise. We would see her often, sketching by the window..."

"What happened to her still haunts us," the man continued, furrowing his brow. "It made us recognize that things like that can happen anywhere — even in a place filled with love."

"Did you see her that night of the art show?" Ruby pressed, her heart pounding. "Anything that might have stood out?"

After a moment of silence, the woman said, "We were here, and we saw a nervous young man leave, someone Emma had been speaking to earlier. He was seen moving erratically, but Emma seemed nonchalant." She paused, her voice wavering. "They had fun at first, but there was something unnerving in his gaze."

"What did he look like?" Liv asked, her eyes widening with eagerness.

"Average build, but wore a black jacket and had shaggy hair. That wasn't the first time we'd seen him, either." The man's forehead crinkled. "I saw him a few days before in a different context... Near the gallery, pacing outside."

The couple's words formed yet another link in the chain of memories — a nerve-racking connection Ruby had long hoped to uncover. "Thank you for sharing that!" Ruby said genuinely. "This is extremely helpful. Every little detail adds to the bigger picture."

As they moved away from the couple, Ruby had an idea. "We should report this. All of these details are critical to reconstructing the night of Emma's disappearance. Each person's memory adds layers to her story."

"Let's write everything down," Bella suggested, pulling out her notepad to jot down notes. "We'll assemble the pieces, make a timeline, figure out who to reach out to next based on what we've uncovered."

"I feel like we're getting somewhere!" Liv smiled. "This is so exciting. We've connected with people who knew her and heard their perspectives. It's only a matter of time before we find something more."

As they settled back into their booth, the weight of shared anecdotes hung in the air—a magnetic surge of individual pathways colliding around a shared memory.

The café was not just a backdrop but a living witness to Emma's existence, each corner filled with shards of her life.

Feeling pulsations of hope coursing through them, Ruby glanced around, realizing their connection to the café was more profound than mere patrons enjoying coffee; they were diggers, seekers of truth hoping to restore order to a life full of silence.

As they were discussing the next round of questions to tackle, Eva approached once more. "You know, if it helps, I can talk to a few customers regularly and see if I can jog their memories. Sometimes familiarity can stir emotions that reveal all sorts of truths," she said with sincerity.

"Thank you, Eva!" Ruby replied, her heart swelling with gratitude. "It would mean a lot to us."

As they finalized their plans to dig deeper into the past, the bustling café transformed into a sanctuary where they could explore the lingering questions. Emma's laughter echoed through their hearts and minds. Each piece of information was becoming like threads interwoven into a tapestry—a vibrant picture that painted a clearer narrative of who Emma was.

Filled with the promise of an unfolding narrative, Ruby knew with certainty: together, they would illuminate the shadows of memory, coaxing the truth of lost time into the light. The café connection now held more significance than they had anticipated; it was a bedrock for investigation, an anchor in the fabric of their journey into the past.

CHAPTER 7

Doubts and Dilemmas

As the sky outside dimmed to a soft twilight, Ruby, Bella, Liv, and Jace continued their investigation in the familiar comfort of the café. The energy they had felt earlier in the day began to shift, tension hovering in the air like an uninvited guest. They gathered at their booth, their earlier excitement dimming as reality settled in; they had hit a brick wall.

Tired but resolute, Ruby traced her finger along the edge of the table, staring at the photograph of Emma's art piece they had printed and posted online. Despite their determination, the responses had trickled in slowly, barely moving the needle of progress in their investigation. Each unanswered message felt like a small weight dragging them down.

"I thought when we posted the photo, it'd create a wave of memories," Liv said, her voice laced with frustration. "But it's been quiet. We've hit dead ends with every lead and everything we thought would be the breakthrough."

"I know," Ruby admitted, her heart heavy as she glanced at Jace, who sat slumped in his seat, his usually bright eyes clouded with uncertainty. "It's like everyone is afraid to discuss what happened... or maybe they've just forgotten."

Jace ran a hand through his messy hair, a gesture Ruby had come to recognize as a sign of his growing tension. "Perhaps digging into the past is stirring up emotions people don't want to face. Emma's disappearance affected this entire community, didn't it?" His voice grew soft, as he wrestled with both determination and despair.

"Or—" Bella drew in a breath, her brow furrowing. "What if we're going about this the wrong way? What if it's not about what people remember but rather about unearthing things they've buried?"

Ruby nodded, but anxiety twisted in her stomach. "But how can we bring up a decade-old tragedy without causing more pain? It's a tight rope we're walking on, and I'm worried we might trigger something darker."

"There's no denying that," Jace replied solemnly. "But we're looking for answers. Answers that could lead us to Emma or at least to the truth. If we don't confront this head-on, will we ever know? Or will we just remain tethered to questions that haunt us forever?"

The conversation turned heavier, silence settling over them. The café was still bustling with life, laughter, and joy, a stark contrast to the shadows creeping into Ruby's thoughts. Surrounded by the familiar warmth of the café, the reassurance that had invigorated them began to fade.

"I just wish we could've talked to Emma," Ruby finally whispered, staring into the depths of her half-empty coffee cup. "It feels like she's slipping through our fingers." A lump formed in her throat as she fought against the ache of longing, wishing for the impossible.

"I can't help thinking, what if we can't uncover the truth?" Bella's voice quivered slightly, echoing the doubt that had begun to tangle with their purpose. "What if we're only digging into a pit of darkness without any light?"

Liv took a deep breath, placing her hand on Bella's. "We wouldn't be here if we didn't want to help Emma. And we owe it to her to keep trying. Maybe there's a different angle we can approach this from. Let's brainstorm all of our connections so far, and see if any threads lead us somewhere new."

"Like what?" Ruby asked, her curiosity piquing slightly amidst the looming fear.

"I mean, look at what we have." Liv pulled out her notebook filled with notes from their conversations, scribbles of memories, and troubling insights. "We've amassed stories from the regulars at the café and learned about that incident outside the gallery. What if we canvassed the surrounding neighborhoods? Talk to shopkeepers, street vendors — anyone who might have glimpsed something that night or even in the days leading up to Emma's disappearance."

"Connecting the dots could provide us a clearer picture," Jace said, his spirit lifting slightly. "Perhaps piecing together the timeline will unveil new perspectives."

"Chatting with local artists might help too," Ruby added, her voice shaking with renewed energy as the idea took hold. "If Emma was an artist, surely she had connections in the community. They could hold valuable insights or even remnants of her art from the show."

"Yes! The artist community is vast and tight-knit," Bella chimed in, a spark of hope igniting in her eyes. "It might be the key we need to unlock the truth about her last days."

With a final gust of determination, Ruby lifted her chin. "Okay, let's commit to this! We can't stop now, not when we've come this far!"

As they reconvened, mapping out their approach for the coming days, doubt began to dissipate, replaced by a simmering desire to uncover the layers shrouding Emma's past.

Yet as they exited the café, Ruby couldn't shake the lingering anxiety that tugged at her heart. The path ahead was still riddled with uncertainty, temptations of doubt creeping in with each step. What if they found something they never wanted to uncover? What if they couldn't bring Emma's story to light?

"How are we going to tackle this?" she pondered aloud, glancing around at the vibrant streets. "What if someone remembers something important but feels too afraid to speak?"

"Then we just need to create a space where they feel safe," Jace replied, his voice steady. "We'll make it clear we're here not to pry, but to understand Emma's story. We want to honor her memory, not unearth wounds."

"Perhaps sharing more of Emma's work might resonate," Bella suggested as they walked briskly toward their first destination. "People might want to share their memories if they feel a connection."

"And using social media could help broaden our reach," Liv added. "Let's encourage the community to share any pieces of art they might have seen or known of—art that might have inspired Emma."

With a renewed sense of commitment, Ruby could feel a shift in the winds of doubt. As they approached the homes lining the city streets, she realized the small moments of connection they had built together could turn into a profound network anchoring them amid the uncertainty.

Surrounded by the excitement of possibility, her friends beside her, doubt slowly melted away. In its place, resolve sparked within her heart, igniting a sense of belief that truth was just beyond the horizon.

Together, they would forge ahead, navigating the labyrinth of memory, intertwining their fates with Emma's story.

And as Ruby held tightly to that hope, she felt a flicker of warmth igniting inside — a whisper promising that, together, they would either uncover light or ignite the dreams of a woman longing to be seen once more.

CHAPTER 8

The Polaroid Connection

The next day dawned with a soft mist clinging to the world, wrapping the city in a gentle shroud that felt both mysterious and comforting. Ruby pulled on her favorite oversized sweater, relishing its warmth against the brisk air that seeped through her window. Today, she had a renewed sense of purpose; she couldn't wait to capture even more moments with her Polaroid camera and see if the magical device could aid in uncovering Emma's story.

As she gathered her belongings, Ruby could hear the familiar sounds of Bella and Liv's banter from the kitchen. The scent of pancakes wafted through the air, mingling with the rich aroma of coffee brewed by Bella, who often fancied herself a budding barista. Joy swelled in Ruby's chest as she realized how lucky she was to have such supportive friends by her side, strangers in their own right but bound by a shared mission.

"Morning, sunshine!" Bella greeted, flipping a pancake with grace. "How did you sleep? Ready for another day of digging through the layers of mystery?"

"Like a rock," Ruby said, her cheeks warming as she helped herself to a plateful of pancakes. "And yes, I can't wait! I was thinking about how we could engage the community more today — maybe even use my Polaroid to spark some connections."

"Great idea!" Liv said, her eyes lighting up. "How about we set up a little pop-up photo booth? You could capture people's portraits, and then invite them to share their thoughts or memories of Emma while they see the picture developing."

Ruby's excitement bubbled over. "Yes! We could position ourselves near the park and invite passersby to join. It could create a space for storytelling, and who knows, we might just stumble upon someone who remembers her!"

"Plus, taking candid shots might encourage more openness. Each photo can act as a bridge, sparking a connection," Bella added, her enthusiasm palpable as she finished plating their breakfast.

After sharing laughter and pancakes, the trio quickly transitioned into planning mode. They sketched out ideas and gathered supplies, including a large corkboard to display photographs, sticky notes for people to write thoughts on, and, of course, Ruby's beloved Polaroid camera.

The sun shone brightly by the time they reached the park, its warm rays piercing through the morning mist and illuminating the vibrant foliage. It was a hub of activity, with families strolling, dogs frolicking, and children laughing. Ruby felt a wave of invigorating energy wash over her — this was the perfect setting to weave stories together.

They set up their makeshift booth beneath the large oak tree that stood majestically at the center of the park. Ruby attached a colorful "Photo Booth for Memories" sign to the corkboard and arranged her camera on a small table. It stood prominently, polished and ready for action, like a treasure chest waiting to incorporate fragments of life into its frame.

As people drifted by, Ruby's heart raced with anticipation. She positioned her camera, a welcoming smile stretching across her face as she beckoned individuals to step forward. "Hey there! Would you like a free portrait? We're gathering memories of a wonderful artist named Emma, who used to frequent this park!"

The first few individuals approached with curiosity. Ruby snapped several candid images — capturing the raw emotions and spontaneity of each moment. Children's laughter, couples stealing glances, and old friends reminiscing flowed through the lens, creating snapshots of humanity woven together by warmth and connection.

"Could we add our thoughts about Emma in this corner?" one woman asked as she admired the setup. She wore an easy smile and held her child's hand, her eyes gleaming with kindness.

"Absolutely! Please feel free," Ruby encouraged, handing her a sticky note and a pen. "It would mean a lot to collect fond memories of her. She was an incredible artist and soul."

As the woman penned her tribute, more individuals began to show interest. The photographs developed slowly in front of their curious eyes, each image blooming into existence like promises of memory being captured in time. The small booth transformed into a hive of storytelling, where laughter intertwined with whispers and warmth, and Ruby felt a charge of hope pulse in her chest.

After taking several photos, she turned to her friends, a blend of excitement and apprehension swirling within her. "What if my Polaroid captures something—some detail that can connect to Emma? Maybe a smile that sparks a memory?"

"That's the beauty of candid photography!" Bella exclaimed passionately. "By preserving these moments, you create threads of connection. Those connections could potentially uncover something for our investigation."

"Let's keep it up, then!" Liv cheered, encouraging the steady flow of visitors.

Two hours passed blissfully, laughter resonating from the booth as Ruby snapped one whimsical photo after another. Each photograph brought forth memories and stories revealing Emma's essence, paving a way to uncover the threads that created her world.

As the sun began to dip lower, Ruby noticed a slight commotion near a cluster of older patrons seated on a nearby bench, their conversation animated and urgent. Curiosity ignited, Ruby excused herself and wandered over, hoping to gauge the exchange.

"Did you hear what they said about that woman from ten years ago?" one elderly gentleman exclaimed.

"She had the most captivating smile. I still see it when I close my eyes," a woman replied, her voice quavering with emotion.

Ruby's heart raced at the mention of Emma's smile. She carefully moved closer, eager to hear more of their conversation. "Excuse me," she interrupted gently, "I couldn't help but overhear. Are you talking about Emma?"

The older gentleman turned toward her, his eyes wide with curiosity. "Yes, dear. She was a wonderful artist! We often saw her sketching in the park. A tragedy took her from us — so sudden. A real gem lost too early."

"Do you have any stories? Memories you would like to share?" Ruby prodded with all the warmth she could muster.

The woman's expression softened, and she nodded slowly. "Emma used to come here nearly every weekend. She would breathe life into her art, drawing inspiration from this very park. There was a festival once—she painted a mural on the community wall down near the river. It was magnificent."

"The mural!" Ruby repeated excitedly. "Did she leave anything hidden in that piece? Did it hold specific meaning?"

The man leaned closer, as if about to share a secret. "There was something about it, something underneath. Emma always had little stories woven into her works. She believed art was a conversation that transcended the visible—some thought she hid personal symbols that connected to experiences... But I could never decipher them all," he admitted.

Ruby's heart raced. "Do you think those elements could have anything to do with what happened to her?"

"I can't say, but if anyone knew, it was her," the woman said with a sigh, her voice layered with sorrow. "Look, get your friend to take a photo of us. I'd love to capture this memory, just like Emma would have."

At that moment, Ruby felt a rush of hope. "Of course!" She rushed back to the booth, her heart pounding. "I'll grab my camera!"

As she focused through the lens on the group of patrons, she couldn't shake the thrill coursing through her. This could unlock something crucial in their journey to honor Emma's memory, perhaps leading to more clues.

After capturing the moment, Ruby took a deep breath, sensing the air shift around them. She'd fostered connections capable of breathing life into the hunt.

"Those memories are flowers growing out of the cracks," she thought, as she rejoined Bella and Liv at their booth, showing off the developed snapshots. "We're closer than ever!"

As the sun sank lower into the horizon, the colors of the park deepened, the golden light casting elongated shadows. The day had blossomed into something beautiful, and Ruby felt a resonance within her Polaroid camera — it had been their silent companion, transforming fleeting moments into treasures.

When Ruby finally returned to the table with the new photos, she looked down at the smiling faces captured on film, brimming with hope and innocence. "I don't think we're just capturing memories. I think we're creating a tapestry of Emma's existence from this past. The Polaroid can reveal so much."

Her friends gathered around, eyes glistening with excitement. "What if we create a display showcasing Emma's memory using these snapshots? We could add people's reflections from today and tie it back to her artwork. This could turn into an exhibit," Bella said, her brow lined with inspiration.

"That is perfect!" Ruby exclaimed, her heart swelling with gratitude for her friends. The idea felt like a beacon, guiding them through the shadows.

The Polaroid connection had sparked not only new memories and ideas but also deeper ties to their mission. Armed with hope and creativity, they would build a bridge between the past and present, and help Emma's voice shoot through the whispers of time.

As the sun dipped below the horizon, painting the sky with hues of orange and purple, Ruby felt a wave of comfort wash over her. She once again saw that beneath the layers of uncertainty, beneath the shadows lurking in the background, were countless stories waiting to be told. And thanks to her camera, they would start to unravel them one snapshot at a time.

CHAPTER 9

A Dark Turn

As the sun slipped below the horizon, the park was slowly enveloped in shadows, casting a tranquil but haunting atmosphere. Ruby, Bella, Liv, and Jace gathered their materials, packing up the remnants of their pop-up photo booth. They had spent a fruitful day collecting memories and stories about Emma, and with excitement in their hearts, they were eager to piece together the narrative that was beginning to form.

"Let's meet tomorrow to organize everything from today," Ruby suggested, her eyes sparkling with enthusiasm. "We can start creating that exhibit for Emma that we talked about. Every memory we captured today deserves a place in this story."

After tossing their collected prints into a cardboard box, they made their way out of the park, their footsteps grazing the pavement, laughter mingling with animated chatter that echoed through the evening air. Yet, as they strolled down Maple Street toward the café, a switch flicked within Ruby, the air laden with unshakeable tension.

An evening chill crept in, seeping into their bones. Ruby's senses heightened, yet she couldn't can shake the feeling that something intangible loomed around them. Perhaps it was anxiety about the investigation pressing down on her; perhaps it was the faintest whisper of something darker lingering in the past.

Just then, Jace halted, his expression shifting. "Do you guys feel that?" he questioned, glancing around as if probing the shadows lurking between the streetlights. "It's like the city is… holding its breath."

Liv shivered. "Yeah. There's a heavier tension in the air tonight."

As they turned a corner, Ruby caught sight of a figure standing unnaturally still at the edge of the alleyway. The distant glow of a streetlamp illuminated a hooded figure, casting a long shadow along the ground. They seemed to be watching the group intently.

"Is it just me, or does that person look familiar?" Bella murmured, uneasiness creeping into her voice. Ruby's heart raced as she squinted, searching for recognition.

Jace shifted nervously but took a step toward the figure. "Hey! Excuse me!" he called out, an undeniable urgency in his tone.

There was no response from the figure, who remained motionless, save for a slight twitch of the hood as if they were contemplating whether to reveal themselves.

"Maybe we should keep walking," Liv suggested hesitantly, her instincts flaring up. "This doesn't feel right."

But before Ruby could say anything, the figure turned slightly, the shadows displacing just enough for Ruby to catch a glimpse of a familiar face — the elusive shadow from the photograph at the café, the same man Jace had described as lingering ominously at Emma's art show.

A chill chased across Ruby's skin. "That's him!" she exclaimed, her voice rising with urgency. "That's the guy we've heard about — the one who was watching Emma."

"Is this a coincidence?" Jace whispered. "Or is he somehow connected?"

In an instant, the stranger's demeanor changed. With a sudden fluidity, he adjusted his hood and stepped into the deeper shadows of the alley, willing to vanish from sight. Ruby, motivated by a mix of fear and determination, dashed forward, nearly drawing her friends along with her.

"Wait!" she cried out, her voice echoing into the night. "We just want to talk! Please!"

But the stranger was faster. He turned on his heel and darted down the alleyway as if he had been waiting for the moment to flee. Jace followed closely behind, his instincts guiding his every step, while Ruby and Liv kept pace, their hearts pounding in sync with their hurried breaths.

"Jace!" Ruby shouted, her voice laced with urgency. "Be careful!"

The figure raced through the maze of alleyways, weaving between buildings, ground crunching beneath their feet. They dodged corners and darted around parked cars, their footfalls echoing against the gritty pavement. Ruby felt adrenaline surging through her as she tried to evade the panic surging within.

"I think I see him!" Jace called out, narrowing his eyes as he brought his determination into focus. "He's heading toward the old factory."

"Let's keep going!" Bella urged, her eyes bright with resolve.

Suddenly, the man stumbled, slipping momentarily against the uneven sidewalk, giving Jace just enough time to catch up. "Stop! We're not going to hurt you," he panted, extending a hand in a mix of plea and authority.

The figure paused, breath hitching as he glanced backward at Jace, caught in the glow of a nearby streetlight. Ruby finally saw his face—a shadow of a man that was unmistakable, a blend of fear and confusion lurking behind haunted eyes.

"Please," the man said, out of breath. "You shouldn't be following me. You have to let it go."

"Who are you?" Ruby pressed, her voice barely containing her urgency. "We need to know—were you at the exhibit? Do you know what happened to Emma?"

A flicker of recognition passed over his features before he shook his head vehemently, panic rising. "You don't understand! You don't know what you're digging into."

"What do you mean? We're trying to honor her memory!" Jace interjected, stepping closer. "We just want answers!"

"Answers?" The man's laughter echoed against the brick walls, but there was no sincerity behind it, only shadows. "Some questions are better left unasked. You're all in danger; you need to back off while you still can."

"Why?" Liv's voice broke through with raw determination. "We deserve to know what happened to Emma! Just tell us!"

But the man shook his head, the fear swirling deeper in his gaze. "Not all lights shine bright, and not everything that disappears is lost forever. Leave this alone; it's not safe for you. You'll find yourself in situations you don't want to face."

With that, he turned away abruptly, fading into the night like a wraith, leaving a chill hanging in the air around them as Ruby and the others stood speechless.

"What in the world just happened?" Bella whispered, her voice trembling.

"I... I don't know," Ruby admitted, her heart racing. "But he was scared. Scared of something that clearly ties back to Emma."

"Why would he warn us about digging deeper if he's involved in all of this? What is he hiding?" Jace questioned, his brow furrowing.

"I don't know," Ruby said. "But we can't back down now. Every warning he gave only makes me want to press on, to uncover the truth—not just about Emma but also about what he's hiding."

They hesitated in the dark, a mix of fear and determination clawing within them. The impact of their encounter left an imprint that echoed in their thoughts, the chilling revelation that shadows were not only linked to Emma but also to the very people trying to find her.

"Let's head back to the café," Liv suggested, her voice steady as she took a deep breath to regain composure. "We need to gather our thoughts before we proceed. Something's brewing beneath the surface, and we're not done yet."

As they walked back through the dimly lit streets, Ruby grappled with the chaos swirling within her. Each heartbeat echoed with questions, fears, and uncertainties.

What did that man know? What secrets lay hidden within the layers they had yet to uncover? The mystery had shifted from a hopeful quest for remembrance to an unnerving journey into the heart of darkness.

One thing was clear: they were pushing into territory that could unravel truths buried deep, and with every step they took into the unknown, they were walking a fine line — a line teetering between discovery and danger.

CHAPTER 10

Family Secrets

The next day dawned gray and heavy, as if the clouds had conspired with the lingering tension from last night's encounter. Ruby woke up with a sense of unease settling in her chest, the words of the hooded stranger reverberating through her mind: "You're all in danger... Not everything that disappears is lost forever." She brushed her hair back, wrestling with a sense of urgency to uncover Emma's truth while combatting her own rising fears.

Her friends arrived shortly after, each wearing expressions of resolve mixed with concern. "Did you sleep at all?" Bella asked, her voice filled with a mix of exhaustion and determination.

"Barely," Ruby admitted, her tone steady in spite of her uneasiness. "But I can't shake the urge to push forward, especially after we ran into that guy. What do you think he meant when he told us we were in danger?"

"I think it's time we dig even deeper," Jace suggested, his eyes scanning the room as if anticipating danger in every corner. "We have to figure out the connections Emma has that might lead us to someone who knows more than we do. What about reaching out to her family?"

"Yes! If Emma had family members who cared for her, they could provide additional insights," Liv chimed in, her fingers fiddling nervously with her notebook. "But we should tread carefully. We don't know how they feel about what happened."

"Right," Ruby nodded, feeling a flutter of apprehension. "Let's not forget that her family might still be grieving and could react defensively."

Bella reached for her phone. "Let's start by doing some research. We need to find out if there are any public records about Emma or her family. Maybe we can locate an address, or even find a way to contact them."

With a shared spirit of collaboration, they huddled around the laptop, embarking on the digital quest to unearth the remnants of Emma's life. Using an array of archives, local newspapers, and social media pages, they began to stitch together the fragments of her past.

After a few hours of digging, they finally found an article published soon after Emma's disappearance, detailing the family's grief and public plea for information. It referenced a family home in the nearby neighborhood, and as Ruby read the intimate details of the article, she felt pangs of sorrow.

"Look at this!" Jace exclaimed, pointing to a paragraph within the article. "It mentions Emma's mother, Lila, and her brother, Kyle. Sounds like they were both incredibly close to her."

"Should we contact them?" Bella asked, lingering over the article. "It might be their first step toward closure or healing."

Ruby hesitated, her heart pounding in her chest. "Yes, but we need to be respectful about how we approach. Maybe we should write a letter, expressing our findings and our intentions. We need to let them know that we want to honor Emma's memory, not disturb what they might want to forget."

After a lengthy discussion, they crafted a letter detailing their intentions and their quest to piece together the truth surrounding Emma's life and her art. Utilizing their collective yearning to seek clarity, they crafted the letter delicately, ensuring it conveyed the utmost respect.

"Alright, it's now or never," Ruby said, her anxiety palpable as they prepared to deliver the letter in person. They bundled up against the brisk weather, all quietly considering the weight of the moment.

As they walked through the neighborhood, Ruby couldn't shake the feeling that they were traversing a threshold into a world marked by grief and unresolved pain. With each step, the fear lingered, growing heavier as they approached the quaint but modest house where Emma had lived.

Standing outside Emma's home felt surreal. The cozy exterior appeared untouched by time and loss; flowerbeds bloomed around the porch, and a gentle breeze whispered through the surrounding trees. Somehow, it felt paradoxically hopeful.

"Here goes nothing," Ruby whispered to her friends, stepping up to the door and knocking gently, her heart racing with anticipation and dread.

The seconds felt like hours, but finally, the door creaked open, revealing a woman whose weary eyes reflected a depth of sorrow that etched itself into her features. Her hair, streaked with hints of gray, framed her face softly, and Ruby could see the flicker of recognition dance across her gaze.

"I'm Lila," the woman said cautiously, her voice barely above a whisper. "Can I help you?"

"We're here about Emma," Ruby stated softly, looking into Lila's hopeful eyes. "We've been gathering stories about her, and we want to honor her memory. We reached out to you because we'd love to talk and hear your thoughts."

Lila's expression shifted, a mixture of pain and hesitation washing over her. "I don't know if talking about her helps," she murmured. "Sometimes, it feels like reopening old wounds."

"I understand," Ruby replied gently, her heart heavy, "but we recognize her as someone extraordinary, and we want to make sure she isn't forgotten. We believe there are people out there who might help us connect pieces of her life that could shed light on what happened."

"Perhaps... I could use some light," Lila said, her voice trembling slightly as she invited them in, stepping aside. "But I haven't spoken about her in ages. My son has also been deeply affected by this... tragedy."

The group exchanged nervous glances before filing into the quaint living room, where memories lingered in every corner, lovingly preserved in family photographs that adorned the walls. Ruby felt the warmth of a past steeped in love, even in the void left by Emma's absence.

"I'll get Kyle," Lila said, breaking the silence. "I think you should speak with him. He might have stories of his own."

Ruby watched her disappear down a hallway, her heart pounding with anticipation. She felt layers of emotion—grief entwined with unresolved questions—hovering in the room. Just then, a young boy entered, eyes wide and curious. He was about seventeen, with tousled hair and an expression that reflected both interest and unease.

"Hey," Kyle said hesitantly, standing with arms crossed. "I heard my mom talking to you. You want to know about Emma?"

"Yes," Ruby said warmly. "We're trying to uncover her story, learn about her passions and her life. She was a remarkable person who touched so many lives."

Kyle shifted slightly, his gaze darting to the floor. "It's hard to think about her. It's like... talking about a ghost."

"I get that," Liv acknowledged gently, trying to create a space where Kyle could feel comfortable. "But she was vibrant, and we want to make sure her light shines on. We have some memories that might help rekindle who she was in everyone's hearts."

As the conversation flowed slowly, Kyle began to open up. "Emma was always lost in her art. She'd tell me that each piece was an exploration of the space between joy and sorrow. She had a way of capturing life's moments like they were frozen in time." His voice cracked slightly.

"What was the last piece she created?" Ruby ventured, her heart aching for the young man's pain.

He paused, memories dancing in his gaze. "It was a mural she painted at 'Canvas & River,'—the people, the colors, the stories. But it's not just her art I miss; it's her laughter. After she disappeared, things became... quiet, you know?" Kyle's voice trembled as he spoke, the weight of pain etched deeply into the line of his jaw.

"She had a friend who started distancing himself shortly before she went missing; I still don't understand why. I feel like that whole situation was just off," he continued, visibly agitated. "I don't want to say too much, but that guy... he had a dark aura."

Ruby exchanged a glance with Bella and Liv. "Do you remember his name? Is he still around?"

"His name was Alex," Kyle muttered darkly, shaking his head. "I don't have all the answers, but I saw enough to know Emma wasn't happy around him. They would argue sometimes, and I... I don't know. I think he had something to do with it." A storm of emotions swirled in his expression.

Ruby's heart thundered, realization dawning. "Was he at the gallery the night Emma disappeared?"

"Yes," Kyle replied, his voice laden with certainty. "He was there. I still see him sometimes, lingering around corners, like he's watching. It makes me feel sick."

Ruby felt the churn of unease grow within her. "Is there any way we can find him? If you feel he's hiding something, then he might lead us closer to the truth."

"I don't know where he hangs around," Kyle said, frustration leaking into his voice. "But trust me; he's no good."

Lila returned to the room, her eyes inquisitive as she sensed the escalating tension. "What's happening?"

"We're trying to piece together Emma's last days, and Kyle's been sharing some vital information," Ruby said, her heart racing as she relayed what they had learned. "He mentioned a friend named Alex. He might be connected to Emma's disappearance."

"Alex?" Lila's voice fell. Her expression turned to one of recognition mixed with dread. "I had always known something was off about him. I'd heard the fights and knew

Emma was becoming emotionally withdrawn. I should have stepped in."

Kyle averted his gaze from his mother, the air thick with an unspoken burden, secrets that had long haunted them.

"This makes sense," Ruby said slowly, piecing together fragments of the unfolding narrative. "If you have any way of reaching him, we need to—"

Before she could finish, Lila interjected, "There might be something in Emma's old belongings that you can look through. Perhaps you might find records, letters—something that connects the dots we've missed."

Hope surged through Ruby as Lila led them to a small room filled with remnants of Emma's life. Sunlight poured through the window, illuminating art supplies, sketch pads, and memory boxes that held whispers of the artist Emma once was.

"I haven't dared to go through her things since she disappeared," Lila's voice quivered with vulnerability. "But maybe it's time we unearth her life instead of letting it fade."

The group nodded, determination flooding their hearts as they began sifting through the treasures of Emma's past. They unfolded crumpled sketches, pages filled with intricate designs, and letters addressed to friends with heartfelt words spilling from her soul.

"Look at this," Liv breathed, holding up a sketch that mirrored the mural Emma had painted—a captivating depiction of a river flowing seamlessly through different landscapes, each one representing a fragment of Emma's emotions.

"It's beautiful!" Ruby exclaimed, her heart leaping as the intricate details caught the light. She turned the page to see a note penned in delicate handwriting: "In the flow of the river, all stories intertwine. I want my art to be a bridge, connecting all who have wandered."

"This could be a significant piece of art linking to Emma's narrative," Bella murmured, her eyes wide as she absorbed the words.

In the corner of the box, Ruby found a folder, its contents spilling over the edges. As she carefully sifted through the documents, a photograph slipped out, revealing a familiar face — the dark-eyed man with shaggy hair, the last image capturing his gaze even as Emma stepped forward.

Her pulse quickened as she flipped it over to find a scribbled note on the back: "A piece of the puzzle, Alex. We must stay cautious; darkness lingers at the edge of the river."

"What?" Ruby whispered, her heart racing at the weight of the implications. "We need to learn more about Alex and how he fits into this intricate web."

With newfound urgency and a spark of fear blurring the edges of hope, they huddled closer, desperation igniting within. The revelation that Alex was involved as a key figure connected to Emma's life set the stage for an even deeper investigation.

Family secrets—hidden pieces buried in memory—were beginning to resurface, and Ruby understood as they sifted through Emma's past that it was time to confront those dark corners, to emerge into the light. Emma's life was worth reclaiming, and Ruby would stop at nothing to uncover the truth buried within the shadows of their intertwined fates.

Chapter ii

The Gallery

The morning sun cast golden rays across the city, illuminating the streets as Ruby, Bella, Liv, and Jace made their way back to Canvas & River, the gallery where Emma had displayed her art years ago. The day felt heavy with purpose, each step resonating with the weight of their investigation. Armed with the revelations from their conversation with Lila and Kyle, the prospect of uncovering more about Emma's past loomed large in their minds.

"Are we ready for this?" Bella asked, her voice reflecting a mix of excitement and hesitation as they approached the gallery's entrance.

Ruby took a deep breath, feeling the familiar surge of adrenaline. "We have to be. Every clue leads us closer to understanding what happened to Emma," she replied, determination lacing her words.

As they stepped inside, the scent of fresh paint mingled with the mellow notes of jazz music playing softly in the background. The space was tranquil, adorned with vibrant artwork that spoke of life, emotions, and narratives that danced in the air. Ruby felt the atmosphere wrap around her like a warm embrace, but beneath that warmth lay a restless energy, a sense of purpose driving them forward.

"Let's find Eva first and see if she can shed more light on Emma's last exhibit," Jace suggested, scanning the gallery for the barista who had previously offered valuable insights.

They meandered through the space, admiring the art on display. Each piece seemed to tell its own story, a reminder of the power of creativity, and Ruby couldn't help but imagine the impact Emma's work had left behind. Finally, they spotted Eva, carefully arranging a new exhibit in the far corner.

"Eva!" Ruby called, waving her hand as they approached. The barista looked up and met their eyes, her face breaking into a welcoming smile.

"Back so soon? You made an impression yesterday," Eva said playfully, brushing her hands on her apron before stepping closer. "Is there more information you've uncovered?"

Ruby hesitated for a moment, gathering the courage to reveal their deeper motivations. "Actually, yes. We spoke with Emma's family, and they shared insights that have led us to believe Alex was involved in her life around the time she disappeared."

Eva's demeanor shifted, her expression sobering as she processed the information. "Alex? I haven't thought about him in years. If he was part of her life, he might have something significant to share. But he was always a bit of a wildcard. Didn't seem to fit with the people Emma usually surrounded herself with."

"No one seemed to want to risk running into him, and I definitely understand that," Jace admitted, crossing his arms. "But we need to know his connection to Emma, especially regarding her art and those last few days."

"I'm curious if anyone still keeps in touch with him," Bella added quietly, her brows knitted with concern. "It might help us piece together the puzzle."

"Why don't you check with the staff? Perhaps they have something on file or might have seen him around," Eva suggested. "And if you need, I can look for more details about Emma's last exhibition, track down any correspondences or records that relate to Alex."

"Thank you!" Ruby replied, a spark of gratitude igniting in her heart. "Any information could lead to something we haven't considered yet."

As they thanked Eva, they split up. Ruby, Bella, and Liv searched for any employee who might remember details surrounding Alex, while Jace promised to help Eva dig through records from Emma's last exhibit, searching out any breadcrumbs that might lead them to answers.

"Remember, we're piecing together something that belongs to Emma," Ruby said quietly, as they approached a group of gallery employees. "But we need to be careful how we position our inquiries. Alex has shadows lurking around him, and we don't want to raise any unnecessary alarm."

"Understood," Bella replied, her voice resolute.

They approached a gallery assistant named Mia, a young woman with painted nails and an eye for detail, who stood beside an array of new artwork displayed on easels. "Hi! We're looking for information on a former artist named Emma who exhibited here a few years back," Ruby began, gauging Mia's reaction.

"Oh, I remember Emma! Everyone loved her work; it was vibrant and emotional," Mia said, her eyes brightening slightly. "What do you need to know? Her last exhibit was unforgettable."

"Well, we're trying to piece together the story of her life and what happened in the days leading up to her disappearance," Ruby explained. "Did you know if she had any particular connections to a guy named Alex?"

Mia's expression darkened momentarily, the shift barely noticeable but impactful nonetheless. "Oh, Alex... That guy was a bit strange. I remember he showed up at the gallery with Emma once in a while, but they seemed to step back and forth between being friends and strained acquaintances. He had this aura that put people off."

"What did you mean?" Bella asked, leaning in closer. "Did he behave unusually?"

"He was unpredictable," Mia continued, her tone laced with hesitation. "While Emma flourished in creativity, Alex often slipped into darker moods—jealousy, antagonism. And each time he appeared, the energy within the gallery changed. Other artists even felt uncomfortable with how he evaluated their work. It's hard to articulate... but it felt like he belittled the art more than appreciated it."

"Were you here the night of her exhibit?" Ruby asked, her heart racing. "Did you see anything out of the ordinary?"

"Yes," Mia admitted, glancing around as if checking for eavesdroppers. "He was here. And there was a confrontation. I overheard them arguing in the back—they were discussing something personal. It didn't seem about art, and their tone escalated quickly."

"What happened?" Ruby pressed, desperation creeping into her voice.

"I didn't get the whole story, but it was like a thunderstorm brewing. I didn't want to pry or get involved. I remember checking on a different section of the gallery, and when I returned, they were gone. Emma was insistent on putting distance between them after that, but I could tell she was shaken."

"When was this?" Jace's voice interjected, having joined the group just in time to catch the tail end of Mia's story.

"All I remember was the swirl of the crowd. That night was chaotic. I don't think I ever saw Emma after that," Mia said softly, an air of sadness washing over her. "And when she vanished, it left a scar, not just on her family but on this entire community."

Gazing at one another, Ruby felt the weight of unresolved fear settle deeper in her heart. "What about the gallery? Is there any way we could see the records of that night? Any photos of who was present or information on Emma's work?"

"Sure, we keep records for every event," Mia said. "Let me check what I have archived."

As Mia disappeared into another section of the gallery, Ruby glanced at her friends, her heart racing at the mounting unraveling of information. "This could lead us to the truth."

After a few minutes, Mia returned, but her expression was grave. "I've come across a few photos from that night. However, there are gaps in the documentation... unwanted evidence and unrecorded accounts of people, like witnesses who might have left early."

Ruby nodded, feeling the weight of the missing pieces missing but also the unique buzz of hope. "We have to gather what we can. Every detail matters."

Mia handed them a folder containing small photographs of various patrons from the event — their faces sharp and vibrant, preserving moments frozen in time. Among them, Ruby's heart skipped a beat as she spotted a photo of Alex, unmistakable with his shaggy hair and dark attire standing near the back of the gallery.

"There he is," she murmured, pointing to the photograph while her friends crowded around her. "We need to know why he was there and what truly happened that night."

As they continued to sift through the photographs, Ruby felt pieces of a puzzle begin to align — connections forming in her mind as if by a magical force, illuminating the shadows veiling Emma's story. They shuffled through interactions, recorded moments unfolding photograph by photograph.

Just then, Mia leaned closer, her eyes narrowing on a particular photo — a snapshot of Emma standing proudly beside her artwork in an animated conversation with a group of people, her smile radiant, her soul palpable. "You know, that looks similar to the mural she painted at the festival. It was, like, her way of connecting elements of our stories together. She believed art could heal."

Ruby's breath caught in her throat, and she felt a swell of emotion welling up inside her. "We have to honor her life through this art — we must share her legacy with everyone who loved her."

The gallery, once filled with vibrant energy, became a sanctum of revelation, a hallowed ground where they could bear witness to Emma's existence — a place where stories from the past finally began to resurface, promising bridges across time.

With every piece they uncovered, brighter pathways connected them all. "Thank you, Mia," Ruby said, her voice thick with gratitude. "We'll return with more hopes of discovering who Emma was and how we can help."

As they exited the gallery, the shadows of the city hung around them, but there was hope igniting within Ruby's chest. They were forging forward in their quest to unearth Emma's truth, and as long as they remained united, they would shine a light upon the darkness that seemed to surround her story.

CHAPTER 12

The Story Behind the Frame

The sun rose on a crisp morning, illuminating the city in vibrant hues of orange and pink, as if the world was awakening from a long slumber. Ruby, Bella, Liv, and Jace gathered in Ruby's small apartment, buzzing with anticipation. The revelations from their trip to Canvas & River the previous day had stirred a collective sense of purpose, pushing them all to dig deeper into Emma's story.

"Okay, let's go through everything we have," Ruby said, spreading out the collection of photographs and notes they had gathered during their investigation on the coffee table. The warm light streamed in through the window, casting a golden glow on their makeshift work area.

"I haven't been able to stop thinking about that photo of Emma and Alex we found," Bella said, tapping the edge of the table. "Do you think they got along? Or was there something darker lurking beneath the surface?"

"Emma always had a way of attracting people," Liv mused, her eyes tracing the edges of the photographs scattered before them. "She wanted to understand lives beyond her own. But I can't shake the feeling that Alex was not who he appeared to be."

"I feel the same," Ruby added, a frown creasing her forehead. "His presence seemed to cast a shadow over her light. Just like Mia suggested, his unpredictability could have played a role in her withdrawing emotionally."

"There might be more to uncover about that dynamic," Jace interjected. "Alex being there that night could be crucial, but it's also important to consider the positive influences in her life. We still need to hear more from her family. Their perspective is potentially invaluable."

"True," Ruby replied, her heart racing at the thought of reaching out to Lila and Kyle again. "We need to connect the dots and learn how their stories intertwine with Emma's. They could bring clarity to the questions we still have."

As they continued sifting through the photos, Ruby's fingertips brushed against one particular image — a candid shot she had taken during their pop-up photo booth in the park. In the background stood an older man staring at Emma's mural in the distance, captivated. The angle was perfect, framed by the autumn leaves, soaking in the warmth of the sun.

"Who is that?" Liv asked, her curiosity piqued as she leaned closer to inspect the photograph.

"I have no idea," Ruby admitted, squinting at the image. It was a fleeting moment, but there was something about the man's expression that implied he held answers to questions she hadn't thought to ask. "Should we look into who he is?"

Jace nodded, his brows knitting together thoughtfully. "If he was drawn to the mural, he might hold a piece of Emma's story. Let's try to see if any local artists or patrons recognize him."

"I'll post this photo on our investigative page," Bella suggested, shuffling through her belongings to grab her phone. "Let's cast a wider net. Maybe he visits the park often and can be identified."

As Bella set to work on spreading the word, Ruby felt the sparks of inspiration ignite her imagination. "What if we organized a small gathering at the park?" she proposed. "Invite people to come together, bring their stories about Emma — have them share and reminisce. It could be a way to honor her memory collectively, and perhaps the man we captured in the photo will join us."

"Yes! That blends beautifully with the goal of creating an exhibit," Liv said enthusiastically. "It's not only about finding answers. It's about healing and remembrance. We want people to reflect on Emma's life and art."

"Let's pin down a date for the gathering," Jace suggested, his eyes sparkling with excitement. "The more individualized the personal stories, the clearer the narrative could become."

With that, they began brainstorming specifics, choosing a date two weekends from that day to give them ample time to spread the word and gather memories. Ruby found herself caught up in thoughts of how making meaningful connections could open doors to new insights about Emma, reigniting a flicker of hope in her heart.

"Now, what about that photograph with Alex?" Ruby asked as Lila's and Kyle's insights continued to resound in her mind. "We should have a conversation with them before we go forward with this gathering. They might help us shed more light on Emma's past relationship with Alex."

"Let's do it," Bella agreed, her fingers working deftly across her phone screen as they confirmed plans for their future gathering.

After they wrapped up their discussions, Ruby gathered with Liv and Jace to prepare for the impromptu visit to Lila and Kyle's home. Once they arrived, Ruby felt a familiar mix of excitement and apprehension overtake her.

The door opened slowly, revealing Lila, her face etched with warmth and curiosity. "You're back! Come in," she welcomed, ushering them into the cozy atmosphere of her home, the lingering sense of nostalgia evident in the air.

"Thank you for having us," Ruby said as they settled into the familiar living room, brimming with mementos from Emma's life and art. "We wanted to follow up on our last conversation."

"I was just thinking about you lot," Lila replied with a touch of a smile. "You're doing something special for Emma. It's helping me too—her memory had begun to feel distant. You've sparked something in me."

"We wanted to ask you and Kyle if you'd be willing to share more about Emma's life leading up to her disappearance," Ruby ventured carefully, her heart racing with anticipation.

Lila's features softened. "Of course. What do you want to know?"

"What kind of relationship did Emma have with Alex?" Jace asked, drawing connections deeper with each question. "Was it ever serious?"

"I've never liked him," Lila replied with a sigh; her voice was marked by a heaviness. "But Emma, she always wanted to see the best in everyone. Alex came into her life shortly before she vanished, and while it might have seemed like an innocent friendship, I knew something was off about him. I warned her, but she was determined to include him in her world."

89

"She cared for her friends profoundly," Kyle added, his posture rigid as he echoed his mother's sentiment. "But I felt like she unwittingly sheltered him—he felt like a leech that began to suck the joy out of her."

Ruby took a deep breath, weighing their words. "We found a photograph of Emma with Alex during her last exhibition. It confirms he was there. Do you think it's possible the dynamic between them played a role in what happened to her?"

Lila looked at Ruby intensely, pain shadowing her eyes. "I felt distrust toward Alex; he never gave me a good vibe. I saw how Emma would light up near friends, but with him, there was always a shadow lurking in the background. When I think back, I wonder if I could've done more—asked Emma not to see him."

Kyle shifted in his seat. "There was a time I saw them arguing. It was in the alley behind the gallery when she thought no one was watching. I could feel the tension from quite a distance. I overheard just a few words, but I never confronted her about it because she seemed to be managing okay."

"What was the argument about?" Ruby asked, trying to pull more information from the seams of their memories.

"I can't say for sure," he replied, disappointment lacing his tone. "But it seemed personal. Perhaps she was reconsidering their friendship."

Lila's eyes narrowed as she mused. "She was an artist, after all. Self-doubt can creep in easily, especially with the pressures of showcasing to others."

The weight of their conversation hung heavily, each word filled with unspoken emotion. "Do you have any old letters or journals from Emma that could shed light on her state of mind?" Ruby asked, hoping to uncover more threads that connected her to Alex and to herself.

"She kept some journals," Lila replied, her voice cracking as she considered the prospect of opening old wounds. "They're in her room—things that can reveal her struggles, dreams, and aspirations… They might even hint whether she confided in anyone about her feelings toward Alex."

"I'd like to see them," Ruby said softly, her heart aching for Emma. "If we can know what she penned during challenging times, it might prove invaluable in helping us understand her more fully."

"Please be gentle; I haven't stepped foot in her room since she vanished," Lila pleaded.

With a nod, Ruby led the way, the echoes of the past whispering to her as they descended the hallway toward Emma's sanctuary. The door creaked open, revealing a room that was a vibrant reminder of a life filled with creativity and dreams.

The pastel colors of the walls radiated warmth, and everywhere Ruby looked, remnants of Emma's passion adjoined with hints of nostalgia. Canvases adorned with sketches hung from the walls, mingling with photographs of friends and family—capturing laughter frozen in time.

"There they are," Lila said, her voice quavering as she gestured toward a wooden desk cluttered with supplies, hastily arranged but possessing an air of serenity. Amidst the bits and bobs, Ruby spotted a notebook tucked beneath a colorful scarf, illuminated by the faint sunlight streaming through the window.

As she picked it up and opened it, a sense of anticipation washed over Ruby. Flipping through the pages, she brushed aside sketches until her eyes landed on Emma's recognizable handwriting, flowing with passion and emotion.

"This is it," Ruby murmured, her heart racing as she scanned entries, each revealing fragments of Emma's thoughts. "Maybe there are insights hidden in these writings that could guide our understanding."

The room fell quiet as Ruby began to read aloud snippets of Emma's reflections. "I struggle to weave my emotions into my art—moments of joy entwined with the shadows that linger." She paused, glancing at Lila and Kyle, who absorbed each word with intensity. "She felt the burden of expectation; there was a search for balance."

As Ruby continued reading, Emma's hopes and fears came to life. The words painted a vivid picture of a young woman grappling with her emotions, striving for acceptance while feeling the stirrings of discontent in her life.

And then she stumbled upon a passage that made her heart stop: "There is someone who appears when I paint—a darkness I can't shake. It's simple; he doesn't belong in my light, but there's a magnetic pull."

Ruby's heart raced as she looked up at Kyle and Lila. "This could be about Alex. She sensed something was wrong."

Lila's expression mirrored her feelings of devastation mixed with realization. "I should have recognized these signs, should have done more… but Emma was never one to lay her burdens on others." Her voice trailed off, a tremor echoing in the silence.

"We didn't know," Kyle interjected, anger flashing in his eyes. "None of us did—she was too busy worrying about keeping everyone else afloat."

As Ruby penned the notes and read various passages aloud, she began piecing together Emma's emotional journey, her art, and the challenges she faced. Each word, each phrase painted a larger picture of a girl seeking purpose in a world where the shadows closed in around her.

"This is about more than just art," Ruby finally said, her voice rising with fervor. "This is about reclaiming Emma's story and confronting the shadows that lingered in her life."

Lila nodded vigorously. "You're right. It's time to bring her narrative into the light, to honor her life in the best way we can."

With renewed energy, they carefully placed the notebook back on the desk, recognizing that Emma's thoughts were now more than just words. They existed as a testament to her rich, yet complicated life—a roadmap for uncovering pieces of her story that remained shrouded in darkness.

As they exited Emma's room, Ruby felt a mix of sadness and gratitude swell in her chest. Every detail they uncovered brought them one step closer to honoring her memory, guiding them toward the truth.

"We have to confront Alex," Ruby declared, her voice steady but filled with determination. "It's time to draw out the darkness and force it into the open."

And with that, their mission was clear—they would not only find the pieces of Emma's past buried in the shadows but also bring light to the truths that had long been hidden behind a frame.

CHAPTER 13

Chasing Shadows

The following day in the cafe, Ruby, Bella, Liv, and Jace gathered around a table adorned with their collected findings, excited yet anxious about the next steps they had to take in their quest to uncover Emma's story and confront the shadows that lingered around her disappearance. Bright sunlight streamed through the large windows, casting playful patterns on the table, providing a stark contrast to the serious nature of their investigation.

"Are we really sure about confronting Alex?" Liv asked, resting her elbow on the table, her brow furrowed with concern. "He sounds unstable, and I can't shake this feeling that there's danger lurking there."

Ruby took a deep breath, steeling her nerves. "I know it's risky, but he was a significant part of Emma's life, and right now, he feels like the only link we have. The note Emma wrote about a 'magnetic pull' to him worries me, and I need to face the other side of this."

Bella tapped her fingers on the table, her energy palpable. "There's strength in numbers. If we go in as a team, we'll be less vulnerable. Plus, we have the evidence from her journals. We just need to keep emotions in check and focus on the facts."

Jace nodded, his eyes filled with determination. "We're only trying to learn the truth. The more we know about Alex and the connection he might have had to Emma's life, the closer we get to piecing the story together."

With their hearts racing and uncertainty gnawing at them, they decided to search for Alex, armed with Emma's journal extracts and the conviction that they owed it to her memory to chase after the shadows hanging over her life.

As they stood outside in the crisp air, Ruby felt apprehensive, but also emboldened by the support of her friends. "We'll start at the café; that's where we last saw him," she said. "After that, we can head to Canvas & River and see if anyone recalls when he was last around."

They moved through the city with determination, feeling the weight of uncertainty yet buoyed by the collective goal of uncovering Emma's truth. The ambiance of anticipation grew as they approached the café, the familiar scent of brewing coffee creating a welcoming yet tense atmosphere.

Once inside, they scanned the bustling crowd, seeking out faces that might provide clues or lead them in Alex's direction. Ruby's heart raced as she caught sight of familiar patrons, hoping that someone might recognize the name they were chasing. The café was alive with chatter, laughter, and the comforting noise that came with a busy midday rush.

"Let's ask Eva if she knows where we might find Alex," Bella suggested, her eyes scanning the room for the barista.

Ruby spotted Eva behind the counter, expertly crafting lattes for the customers. She felt a mix of hope and trepidation wash over her as they approached. "Eva!" she called out, beckoning her over.

Eva wiped her hands on her apron and smiled warmly as she approached. "Hey there! Back again. What can I do for you?"

"We were hoping to ask about Alex," Ruby began, her tone earnest yet cautious. "We're trying to find him since he's been linked to Emma's life before she vanished. I know he used to come here often."

At the mention of Alex's name, Eva's expression shifted, a shadow crossing her face. "Alex," she murmured, almost to herself. "He used to come in here a lot, but like Emma, he seemed to drift away."

"Do you know where we might find him?" Liv asked, her nervous energy bubbling beneath the surface.

Eva scratched her head thoughtfully. "Last I heard, he was spending time around the local art district. He used to hang out with some of the artists there, particularly a few who seemed to resonate with his darker side."

"Do you remember any specific spots?" Ruby pressed, her determination shining through.

"There's this old warehouse turned gallery on Willow Street — it's kind of known as a gathering place for more underground art shows. Alex sometimes graced those events, soaking in the darker energy." Eva gestured vaguely, a twinge of concern evident in her expression. "But just be careful. The art scene there can be unpredictable; it attracts all sorts."

"Thank you, Eva. We'll keep that in mind," Ruby replied, her heart racing with a mix of excitement and apprehension.

After discussing Alex's potential whereabouts, the group decided to head towards Willow Street immediately. The walk to the district felt electric, every sound around them enhancing their nerves as they prepared to confront whatever secrets lay hidden in the shadows.

Arriving at the gallery, Ruby couldn't shake the weight that hung over them. The warehouse exterior loomed large and intimidating, a gray monolith against the vibrant colors of street art that adorned the surrounding area. The atmosphere was laden with an energy that both thrilled and unnerved her.

They shared hesitant glances before stepping inside, the dim lighting revealing a cavernous space filled with eclectic artwork plastered against the walls. From abstract murals to haunting sculptures, the atmosphere was vibrant yet had an underlying tone of chaos.

"Let's split up and blend into the atmosphere," Jace suggested. "We should scout for Alex quietly before making any waves."

As they separated amongst the artwork, Ruby meandered through the maze of displays, her heart pounding in her chest. Each piece beckoned her with emotion, but her focus remained solely on finding Alex. She felt shadows whispering around her, shadows mirroring the stories they sought to illuminate.

After weaving past several installations, Ruby caught sight of a group gathered in the far corner, their voices a murmur beneath the jazz-infused music playing in the background. She approached quietly, her heart racing when she recognized the dark-haired man at the center of the crowd.

It was Alex, his presence unmistakable. Ruby felt a knot form in her stomach as she listened to him engage in intense discussion about art's raw power. His voice, though smooth, had an edge that unsettled her. He couldn't help but command attention as he gestured passionately.

"Art is a reflection of experience, chaos, and freedom — it can harbor pain within joy, much like life itself," he said, the resonance of his words pouring over her like a chill. "Those who don't understand that dance with shadows—they stay blind."

Ruby felt a mix of anxiety and curiosity. Just then, Alex's gaze flicked through the crowd, and she ducked behind a nearby piece of abstract art — a complex interplay of colors that mirrored her own emotions. She had to gather her thoughts and approach at the right moment or risk setting him off.

Gathering courage, she waited patiently until the conversation lulled, then stepped forward, her heart pounding in her chest. "Alex?" she called out softly, feeling the eyes of those around her shift their focus.

He turned slowly, his expression morphing from intrigued to cautious as he regarded her. "And you are?" he asked coolly, maintaining an air of detached curiosity.

"I'm Ruby," she replied, letting determination seep into her voice. "I'm looking for answers about Emma. We need to talk."

The surrounding crowd began dissipating, sensing the tension as curious exchanges murmured across the room. Ruby could feel the air shift, charged with anticipation as she stood before Alex, his figure casting an imposing shadow.

"Talk? About Emma?" Alex scoffed lightly. "What a pleasure to meet someone still holding onto the past. But perhaps you should heed caution, little girl; the past can haunt even the brightest of souls."

His words felt like daggers, and Ruby's resolve hardened. "I'm not afraid of shadows." She refused to back down. "Emma was an incredible artist, and we're gathering stories to honor her memory. But you must be a part of it. You were in her life at a crucial moment — and then she vanished."

Alex's facade slipped for a moment, revealing a haunting shadow behind his eyes. "Vanished? Or escaped from this dull reality? She was plagued with doubts, struggles, the chaos of being a creator in a world that clamors for uniformity. You have no idea what she was wrestling with."

"Then help us understand — what was she dealing with?" Ruby pressed. "What did you mean by your connection? You could help us find answers. We just want to know what happened!"

A fleeting moment of vulnerability crossed Alex's face before it hardened again. "You think you can navigate these shadows with mere curiosity? You hunt for tales of a tragic ending without knowing the full story. What if mixed emotions were part of her artistry? What if she was breaking free?"

"Breaking free from what? From you?" Ruby challenged, sadness creeping into her voice. "She was a light, and you were part of her darkness. If that night in the gallery spiraled into something darker, it is your responsibility to tell us! What really happened to her?"

Alex's demeanor shifted once more, indignant. "You don't understand! People always take what they want from the story, twisting it to fit their narrative, leaving the aftermath for others. Maybe she chose not to be found — a choice that holds its own power."

At that moment, a sense of chaos enveloped the space, as if echoes from the past began to clash with the present. Ruby felt the weight of Emma's story pressing down, the reality of confronting Alex creating a swirling storm of uncertainty.

"Emma deserves more than just a whispered memory," Ruby asserted, her voice unwavering. "If you were a friend, you owe it to her to reveal the truth. Help us connect the dots — it's about time you own up!"

Alex stepped back, his expression betraying a conflict brewing in his heart. An eerie silence stretched between them, punctuated only by the ambient sound of the gallery. Every inch of Ruby's skin tingled with the weight of the moment.

"Consider this closely." Alex turned away slightly, glancing around the gallery, where curious onlookers lingered on edges of the conversations, piquing his discomfort. "If you wish to uncover those shadows, you may need to embrace them. Things can often spiral, even faster than you anticipate. Are you ready for what lies beneath?"

With that, he slipped into the crowd, leaving Ruby standing there amidst the uncertainty. The moment had passed, yet the echoes of his words lingered in the air, thickening the atmosphere with trepidation.

As the crowd broke up and energy around the gallery shifted, Ruby found herself surrounded by her friends, their expressions ripe with concern.

"Well, that didn't go as planned," Jace said, his expression mirroring Ruby's own feelings of bewilderment.

"But it's clear Alex knows something," Bella added, crossing her arms. "He's terrified of facing whatever truth lies within — and yet, he's equally intrigued by the shadows."

"But what does that mean for us?" Liv questioned, her brow furrowing in thought. "Should we pursue him further or take a step back? We might just be chasing deeper darkness."

Ruby stared at the doorway through which Alex had just disappeared, more determined than ever. "We can't let that darkness scare us away. If anything, it might lead us straight to the heart of Emma's truth. The kind of truth that ultimately sets her spirit free."

Feeling the adrenaline surge through her, Ruby resolved to follow this path, undeterred by the shadows that had once haunted Emma. They had begun to unearth the tangled web of connections, and there were still answers waiting to be discovered. With renewed conviction, they made their way out of the gallery, ready to confront whatever shadows stretched beyond the edges of their understanding.

CHAPTER 14

Secrets Revealed

The sky had darkened into a deep navy by the time Ruby, Bella, Liv, and Jace stood outside the gallery, simmering with unprocessed emotions after their encounter with Alex. The tension of the day hung thick in the air, a storm of uncertainty brewing deep within Ruby's heart.

"What do we do now?" Liv asked, her voice laced with a mixture of worry and determination as they huddled together on the sidewalk, the faint glow of streetlights casting gentle shadows around them.

"We need to piece together what we learned from Alex," Ruby replied, feeling the weight of responsibility settle over her. "He left us with more questions than answers, but I can't shake the feeling that he holds the key to understanding what really happened to Emma."

"And we know he's aware of the darkness surrounding her," Bella added, her eyes narrowing thoughtfully. "Maybe he's hiding something that could connect the dots between Emma's life and his own role in it."

"Let's regroup at my place tonight," Jace suggested, a hint of urgency in his voice. "We need to discuss everything we've uncovered and devise a new approach. I think we're close, but there's a missing piece we need to dig into."

The group nodded in agreement as they made their way back to Ruby's apartment. As they settled on the couch, Ruby pulled out Emma's notebook, flipping through the pages filled with thoughts, sketches, and dreams. The weight of the previously hidden words felt heavier now, the knowledge they held seeping into the very essence of their mission.

"Let's start by reviewing the notes we took yesterday," Ruby suggested, her eyes scanning the room for the scattered pieces of their investigation. "Then we can layer in the information about Alex."

Together, they poured over snippets of Emma's reflections. The entries revealed a rich and complex inner world, filled with struggles and triumphs, and Ruby felt her chest tighten with every unspooled word.

"Look here," Bella pointed to one of the entries. "Emma mentions the complexities of friendship. She seems to grapple with her feelings toward Alex—torn between finding acceptance and battling against the unease he brings. Do you think she knew there was more to him?"

"Possibly," Jace said, his brow furrowing as he considered the implications. "It seems clear she sensed something off about it, yet wanted to give him a chance. But the deeper we dig, the more it feels like she might have regretted it."

"Exactly," Liv chimed in, scribbling notes on a sticky pad. "If there's any chance Emma was writing about specific incidents, it's key for us to connect them to her moments of doubt about him."

With a renewed sense of urgency, Ruby turned to the next pages, the cursive dance of Emma's handwriting easing her anxiety. "I also want to touch base with Lila and Kyle," she suggested, shuffling through a few memory cards. "There's clearly more to this story that involves family dynamics. We're uncovering more layers, so let's not forget about those ties."

Jace nodded, a look of contemplation washing over his face. "Family is one thing that can shift everything; their experiences affect how we process relationships and emotions. Emma's family dynamic could reveal something we haven't considered yet."

"I think it's time we confront Alex and bring in the family dynamics," Ruby said, determination flooding her voice. "He may have been involved in Emma's life, but we need to understand how her family viewed him during that time as well."

Bella smiled knowingly, her enthusiasm igniting their motivation. "We can't give this unknown away. Besides, bringing everything together could help us draw out some deeper truths."

As the night deepened, the air around them thickened with the fervor of the inquiry they had begun. Each moment mattered. The shadows felt closer and closer, but sunlight sparkled just beyond; they were destined to navigate through the interplay of light and darkness until they discovered the truth.

The following day, the quartet returned to Canvas & River, hoping to locate Alex and confront him once again. As they entered the gallery, the air buzzed with creative energy; people admired artwork, and the vibe brimmed with possibility. Ruby felt her determination renewed.

"Let's split up and check different sections—he might not be coming back to the same spot," Jace proposed, glancing at the winding hallways filled with new exhibitions.

Ruby nodded, her heart racing as she ventured deeper into the gallery. She scanned the walls and corners with intent — this was no longer simply about tracking down Alex; it was about piecing together a narrative that had been obscured from view for too long.

Lost in a sea of colors, Ruby momentarily lost her train of thought. Then she spotted a small group gathered near an installation featuring Emma's work—a vibrant interpretation of her mural, its colors dancing with life. Ruby felt a pang of both pride and sorrow wash over her as she watched the interaction.

She stepped closer, straining to hear snippets of conversation. "Emma had such a unique perspective," one patron remarked, while others nodded in agreement. "Her work really spoke to the depths of emotion."

"Excuse me!" Ruby interjected, her voice cutting through the chatter. "Do any of you know where I might find Alex? I was hoping to speak with him."

Gasps of recognition rippled through the group, and a woman stepped forward, her eyes widening. "You're looking for Alex? He hasn't been around lately—but I heard he did have some connection to Emma."

"What do you mean?" Ruby pressed eagerly, feeling the tension of anticipation mount.

"The last time I saw him, he was hanging around the art district, speaking gloomily about how he felt tied to the darkness. It's rumored he was working on another project

105

that echoed themes of loss and shadows," the woman explained, her voice laden with curiosity. "But honestly, if you're looking for him, I'd check the old warehouse near Willow Street. People say he tends to gravitate toward places that resonate with eerie energy."

"Thanks for the tip!" Ruby said as the group dispersed, excitement bubbling within her. She quickly regrouped with Bella, Liv, and Jace, updating them about Alex's rumored whereabouts.

"Looks like we're headed toward the warehouse again," Ruby said, determination flooding her voice.

As they made their way to Willow Street, Ruby felt the chill creep in, the shadows thickening around them. They had encountered so much already; every step deeper felt like a plunge into the unknown.

When they reached the warehouse, the atmosphere was heavy, and the once-vibrant street art loomed like ghostly reminders of the lives intersecting within the space. The doors creaked ominously as they pushed them open, revealing a world shrouded in mystery.

Echoing footsteps reverberated against the bricks, as they stepped cautiously inside. Graffiti-covered walls adorned colorful murals in various states of decay, remnants of past exhibitions echoing the essence of creativity that thrived within the darkness.

"Let's split up again," Jace whispered, his eyes scanning the cavernous space. "We should cover more ground."

"Be careful. Keep your phones on and stay within sight of each other," Ruby warned, her heart racing with both anticipation and fear.

As they ventured deeper into the shadows, Ruby's gaze shifted, catching fleeting movements in the corners of her vision. The atmosphere felt oppressive; the air thick with unspoken secrets.

It wasn't long before Ruby rounded a corner and caught sight of a figure painting in the hushed light. She held her breath as the familiar sight of Alex emerged, absorbed in his work, the brush moving with a wild kind of energy.

"Ruby!" Bella's voice broke through the silence, and the three friends joined her in cautiously approaching Alex.

"Alex," Ruby spoke up, resolve coursing through her. "We need to talk."

He paused, his brush hovering above the canvas. "I didn't expect to see you here. Didn't I warn you about delving too deeply into the shadows?" he said, an edge creeping into his voice.

"We can't ignore what's been left in the dark any longer," Ruby asserted, stepping closer. "We want to understand Emma's connection to you."

"Ah, Emma, always seeking light," he said, his tone growing colder. "But she understood the balance between light and dark, didn't she? That's why we had our moments."

"How did she feel about you?" Bella pressed unwaveringly. "What was your relationship like in those final days?"

"You should know," he replied, annoyance creeping into his words. "She didn't want to consider who I was anymore. I lost her to a different world than the one we were building together. But the depths of art can invoke darker emotions."

"Then help us understand," Jace urged, stepping forward. "You may hold the key to uncovering the truth. We aim to honor Emma's memory; nothing more and nothing less."

Alex's shoulders tightened, and though a flicker of vulnerability passed through him, he continued to shield himself behind layers of detachment. "Art is not just a reflection; it can become a trance—a way to push us to the edge. Maybe Emma wanted to escape the pain of feeling."

"By distancing herself from you?" Ruby interjected, frustration rising. "You had the opportunity to build something meaningful. What happened during the exhibition —the argument? What was that about?"

Alex looked away, returning to his painting as if trying to hide behind the strokes of color that he poured onto the canvas. "Her pleading voice was like a weight—a reminder of everything that can shatter beneath the surface. And perhaps that night, it did."

"Why can't you just tell us? Dive into the emotion that drives your creations!" Ruby shouted, feeling frustration bubble over. "You need to reveal your shadows! You owe it to Emma."

For a fraction of a moment, Alex faltered. "I wasn't always the one she meant to have by her side. I had my own darkness, and when she tried to escape, I didn't do enough to hold her back."

"What happened? Did you have a fight?" Liv pressed, her voice steady yet desperate.

Letting go of the brush, Alex finally turned toward them, guarded walls cracking under the weight of his emotions. "She wanted to break free, like I told you. We mixed in circles, created art, but it always felt like losing grip on the world. I feared that distance would breed chaos, and when she lashed out, I recoiled."

Ruby felt a flood of clarity wash over her. "And then what? Did you argue? What did you say?"

"I told her her art wasn't enough. That it wouldn't matter if she was lost to it," Alex admitted, his voice wavering. "The moment I realized I had pushed her into the arms of uncertainty, it felt like the very ground crumbled beneath me. I believed she had fallen into the shadows I'd managed to keep at bay—an act of betrayal turned monstrous."

The weight of Alex's confession echoed in the cavernous space. Ruby felt a swirl of emotions—the anger, sadness, and compassion begging for release. "So you didn't know where she went after the gallery?"

"I didn't know until everything went dark," he whispered, his gaze sinking to the floor. "You all need to understand; I wasn't manipulating her. She was the one who wanted to challenge everything... and part of that darkness was me."

"The tension is deeper than either of us understood," Jace said quietly, a mixture of understanding and sorrow reflected in his voice. "Emma was struggling not just with you, but with herself. How can we navigate this without confronting the tricky edges?"

"I don't believe it was just about me; it was always about her," Alex said, anguish slicing through his voice. "But to find her, you must accept that confronting those shadows may cost you dearly. Are you ready for that?"

The weight of Alex's words hung thick in the air, swirling with all the love and the chaos Emma had once sustained.

Ruby felt a flicker of clarity illuminating the darkness they had all been chasing.

"Understanding and confronting those shadows mean learning from our past," Ruby said softly, her eyes locked onto Alex. "It's about piecing together memories that bring us closer to the truth—for Emma and for ourselves."

The silence draped over them, awkward yet charged with a new potential. They all stood in that dimly lit warehouse, surrounded by the faint echoes of art and the unveiled truths cascading from their words.

Slowly, Ruby could feel the shadows beginning to lift; though they lingered around them, they could finally see a path toward healing and understanding, not just for Emma, but for the fractured pieces of their own lives.

As Ruby exchanged glances with her friends, a collective recognition set in: they would chase the shadows, confront the darkness, and find their way back to Emma's light—a light that, even in its absence, would guide them toward the truth waiting to be uncovered.

CHAPTER 15

Treading Lightly

The air in the dimly lit warehouse was thick with tension as Ruby, Bella, Liv, and Jace stood in the aftermath of their emotional encounter with Alex. Shadows danced along the walls, reflecting the turmoil echoing within the group's hearts. They lingered in the ambiguous space, absorbing the weight of Alex's revelations but feeling the burden of uncertainty pressing heavily on their shoulders.

"Wow," Bella finally whispered, breaking the silence that enveloped them. "I didn't expect that. Alex's admission stirred so many emotions. It feels like we've just touched the tip of the iceberg."

Ruby nodded, her thoughts racing. "It's clear that Emma's struggles were deeper than we realized. She was an artist trying to reconcile her emotions with the world surrounding her—and Alex was a mixed blessing in that relationship. The layers of pain she held… it's overwhelming."

"What I can't shake is that we may have inadvertently put ourselves in more danger," Jace murmured cautiously, his brow furrowed. "We know Alex's influence was not positive, and if he knew how close we were to uncovering the truth… "

"Exactly," Liv chimed in, her tone serious. "We're treading on ground that's unstable. We need to be super cautious about how we approach whatever we find next."

"Agreed," Ruby said firmly. "But we can't lose momentum. If we don't act after learning what we have, then that darkness will continue to haunt us—and Emma's family deserves closure."

"Maybe we should take a day to regroup," Bella suggested. "Can we look into the shadows we've unveiled without risking going too deep too quickly? We might get more intel by gathering outside perspectives. First, let's check back with Lila to see how she feels about Alex's revelations."

They all nodded in agreement, the unspoken pulse of commitment binding them together. Careful steps toward caution had become essential; they balanced the pursuit of truth with the need for prudence.

Later that evening, they found themselves back at Lila and Kyle's comforting home. The familiar scent of fresh coffee wafted through the air, mingling with the warmth of family photographs that adorned the walls. Ruby felt a sense of calm wash over her, the ambiance juxtaposed against the lingering turmoil from earlier.

Lila welcomed them into the living room, her eyes reflecting a newfound resoluteness. "I've been thinking about what you all said regarding Alex. The past has a funny way of tangling with the present, and it's clear he may hold secrets we need to confront."

"Yes, but we also know he may not be a reliable source," Ruby replied cautiously, feeling the weight of the conversation they were about to have. "He's not just Emma's past; he's a complication we may have to navigate carefully to uncover the truth."

"I didn't think I'd ever consider taking that path, but maybe some truths deserve to be chased," Lila said softly, her gaze lifting toward a photograph of Emma displayed prominently on the mantel. "If you believe confronting Alex will lead to something that provides closure… then it's worth exploring."

Ruby exchanged glances with her friends, knowing they were all sensing the gravity of the moment. "Can you tell us more about Alex? Maybe there's more context from your perspective we need to know before we make decisions," she asked.

Lila took a deep breath, gathering her thoughts as she considered how to navigate the murky waters of their discussion. "I remember the first time Emma brought Alex to the house; it was a familiar float between friends. He laughed, he seemed warm—until he started exhibiting behavior that made me question his intentions."

"What did you see?" Liv asked, leaning in closer to capture every word.

"There were subtle shifts," Lila recalled, folding her hands together. "Emma became a bit withdrawn around him. It was as if he siphoned her light when he was in the room. I knew instinctively that I needed to watch him closely. He thrived on the drama—she was a muse to him, not a partner."

"Just like what Mia said about him in the gallery…" Ruby murmured, her heart racing. "But why didn't you step in sooner? Was it simply a matter of that thin line between loyalty and concern?"

Lila sighed heavily, tears glimmering in her eyes. "I thought she had it under control, that she enjoyed the chaos. I didn't want to impose my worries upon her. But now I see those weren't just fleeting feelings; something did linger beneath the surface. It's haunting me. I wish I had been braver, stronger."

"It's not too late," Kyle interjected, his voice filled with determination. "Emma matters. We can confront what needs to be confronted!"

Ruby felt a surge of sympathy toward Lila. "We're going to bring Emma's story to light, but we need your help. If you can share more about the dynamics from your family's perspective, it might provide context we can use to balance confronting Alex without putting any of us at greater risk."

Lila inhaled deeply, blinking back tears. "There have been conversations among family members that I deemed insignificant at the time. Emma's art often mirrored her emotions. Before she disappeared, her work shifted significantly, capturing themes of conflict and shadows dancing around brighter moments; perhaps they reflected her struggles with Alex. But I never saw it until now."

"Can we take a look at her other art pieces? Maybe we'll discover something new," Ruby suggested, her heart racing at the thought.

Lila nodded. "There's a stack of her previous work in the garage. Let's go together; I believe we have some sketches still left over from commissions she didn't finish. They might hold revelations we missed when she left."

With resolute excitement, they all headed to the garage, where remnants of Emma's life resided, each piece waiting to unveil stories lost in time. Ruby was filled with anticipation as they entered the dimly lit space filled with dust and memories.

Finally, they unearthed canvases, sketches, and disconnected art pieces piled neatly against the walls. Ruby felt a shiver of excitement whisper through her as they began sorting through them—each piece was a pulse of Emma's essence, her emotions, and her talent — captured in vibrant brushstrokes that transcended the silence.

The sketches born from Emma's hand came to life, revealing emotions that had simmered beneath every line. Ruby gasped as she stumbled upon a detailed drawing depicting tangled hearts shrouded in shadows under a vivid sun. She turned to Lila. "Did she ever show you this one?"

"Yes! She was frustrated with both the message and how emotions blended with darkness. I could tell she struggled with her connection to Alex even in her art," Lila replied, her voice trembling as a wave of recognition washed over her.

As Ruby continued to dig through the documents, another piece caught her eye. It was a collage filled with photos, printed notes, and sketches of various memories—each image harmoniously intertwined. Among them was a picture of Alex, his face shadowed yet captivating. Ruby felt a surge of excitement and concern.

"Do you remember this?" Ruby asked Lila, holding up the collage.

Lila gasped softly, her fingers brushing the collage as she stepped closer. "Yes! Emma composed this just a few months before... before everything changed."

"Is that a piece of a song written on the edge?" Jace asked, glancing at the edge of the collage.

"I think so," Ruby replied, carefully lifting the collage as curiosity bubbled within her.

Excited, Bella moved in for a closer look. "Let's read what it says. It might hint at something important."

As they inspected the edges, Ruby read aloud: "In this chaos, I reflect with shadows guiding the way. At every turn, the light will chase what lingers; in every struggle, a piece of art shall remain."

Ruby's mind raced, the message holding layers of meaning. "This speaks volumes! She felt the battle between light and darkness. Perhaps it was a physical manifestation of her relationship with Alex and a deeper understanding of her own artistry."

Lila wiped away a tear as she stepped closer to Ruby's side, each word resonating deeply. "She was searching for balance within herself; it's something I hadn't fully recognized until now."

"What if we could analyze the timing of this piece alongside her final days with Alex?" Liv suggested, her energy igniting further excitement. "It could provide insight into her shifting sense of self."

"Yes!" Ruby said, feeling a pulse of inspiration surge through her. "Understanding Emma's emotional spectrum during her last moments could paint the full picture we've been missing. It's all interconnected."

With renewed vigor, they dove deeper into Emma's collection. Each piece revealed fragments of her life, her struggles, and her artistry, creating a vivid landscape that reflected the tension she had faced.

As they began to pack up the art and sketches, Ruby felt a connection blossom among them — a bond ignited deeper with every memory that had surfaced. But as Lila gathered a few more pieces, she paused, her gaze drawn to an untouched canvas leaning against the wall.

"What's this one?" Lila asked softly, stepping forward to unveil the canvas, which appeared draped in a cloth.

Ruby held her breath as Lila uncovered it, revealing a dramatic image: a river depicted in turbulent shades of blue and black, swirling around a bright sun breaking through the clouds. Ruby felt an electric charge course through her, the symbolism striking a chord deep within her essence.

"This was her final piece," Lila murmured, awe and sorrow whispering through her voice. "It was meant for an upcoming exhibit—one that would showcase her growth as an artist."

"What happened?" Ruby questioned gently, her heart racing.

"I was worried she was pushing herself too much once it was processed. She wanted to convey her complexities, but with that drive for perfection came anxiety—so much uncertainty during that time. I fear she might have wanted to explore those darker themes so deeply that she lost touch."

"Or maybe something else drew her in—tangled her inner light with the shadows," Bella offered, her voice quivering.

As they considered the implications of Emma's final piece, the weight of the moment settled in, thick with revelations deeper than they'd ever expected. This journey was revealing more than just Emma's struggles; it explored the relationships that defined her, the art that defined her, and the shadows Alex brought into her world.

"Together, we can create a narrative that captures Emma fully —not just the artist, but the person," Ruby said, determination flooding her voice. "We're treading lightly, but we're also gaining insight, unraveling the depths of her life before she faded into the darkness."

The realization renewed the collective spirit within them, binding them ever tighter, preparing them for the inevitable confrontation with truths aching to be unearthed. The shadows would be chased down, not as a threat, but as a journey filled with purpose and remembrance, leading them to where Emma's legacy deserved to shine once more.

CHAPTER 16

A Breakthrough Moment

The days following their visit to Lila and Kyle's home felt charged with anticipation. Ruby, Bella, Liv, and Jace became increasingly determined to uncover the truth behind Emma's disappearance. The emotional intensity of their recent encounters lingered, each moment building on the emotional foundation they had laid — they were drawing closer to revelations that could illuminate the obscured corners of Emma's life.

Ruby had no idea the extent of the layers they would peel back or what new emotions would tangle together during their journey. In the days since discovering Emma's poignant collage and her symbolic river painting, they had pressed on relentlessly, brainstorming ways to approach Alex again while simultaneously planning the gathering at the park to honor Emma's memory.

Morning light streamed through Ruby's window as she gathered her notes and sketches in preparation for the gathering. They had worked tirelessly to ensure the event would celebrate Emma's legacy, capturing the essence of the artist who had meant so much to those around her.

"Okay, today is the day," Ruby said, glancing at her watch and feeling the excitement bubbling within her. "If we're going to connect with the community, we need to be ready to share Emma's legacy and gather stories that illuminate her life."

As her friends arrived, the energy shifted with their collective spirit, each of them eager to contribute to the gathering that they envisioned as a tribute to Emma's artistry and heart.

"Are we all set with the photos and information from the art exhibit?" Bella asked, glancing over the displays they had set up under the large oak tree in the park.

"Yep! I printed out the collage we found in Emma's room, along with the photos we captured at the café. They'll serve as guiding pieces while reminding everyone of what she meant," Ruby replied, trying to quell her nervousness.

As the hours passed, more and more familiar faces began to appear, the warmth of community enveloping them as they arranged the park. Friends and family of Emma trickled in, their stories ready to intertwine like threads in a tapestry of reminiscence.

"Hello, everyone!" Ruby called out, her heart pounding in her chest as she stepped forward, standing tall amidst the gathering. "We're here to celebrate the life and artistry of Emma. Everyone's contributions, stories, and experiences mean the world to us."

As the sun dipped low in the sky, illuminating the park with a glimmering golden hue, voices began to weave around them. Memories surged forth, each one a brushstroke, piecing together Emma's impact in the lives of all gathered around.

"Emma painted life with such passion," an older woman shared, her voice filled with nostalgia. "Her laughter was nearly infectious! She had a gift for making people feel seen."

Others echoed similar sentiments, sharing moments when Emma had brightened their days or inspired those around her with her art. With every story, Ruby felt a profound sense of unity forming within the gathered crowd.

But as the evening grew darker, and the shadows deepened, questions began to arise.

"Did anyone here know about her relationship with Alex?" Ruby asked finally, her stomach twisting as she braced for the responses.

An uncomfortable hush fell over the crowd, and the hesitant glances exchanged between familiar faces spoke volumes. After a beat, a young man stepped forward, his face pale yet resolute. "I knew Alex. I saw him at the gallery the night of Emma's exhibit. He wasn't in a good place; I could feel the tension in the air."

"What was he like?" Liv asked, her curiosity mingling with apprehension.

"He was always riding the edge. You could see the darkness swimming in his eyes," he replied, shaking his head. "When Emma painted, you could see the joy in her work, but then you'd see him hover—a shadow, draining her light."

Ruby leaned in, her heart racing. "Did you witness the argument they had? Was there anything alarming you noticed that night?"

"I didn't hear the specifics, but I sensed their connection was toxic," the man recounted, his voice trembling lightly. "I saw them arguing outside the gallery just before the exhibit opened. Emma wasn't herself that night—she felt trapped, caught in a web of expectations," he said, eyes drifting down.

The tension in the air thickened as murmurs rippled through the crowd, tension and sadness wrapping around them like a storm cloud. Before Ruby could speak again, another person stepped forward—a woman with striking blue hair, who'd been quietly taking in the conversations.

"I was there that night as well," she said, her voice steady yet layered with emotion. "Emma's passion was truly radiant, but Alex's presence was suffocating. He pulled her aside and started raising his voice. I overheard him mention feelings of betrayal when he saw someone else talking to her. It felt like a confrontation was brewing, but I didn't want to intervene."

Ruby's heart raced, emotions swirling. "Did you see where they went afterward?"

The woman shook her head. "I tried not to pry... it felt private, but when I don't hear from her anymore, I felt something wasn't right. It was like she became lost."

"We've been trying to navigate those shadows," Ruby said softly, feeling the empathy of the gathering strengthen. "But we can bring her story back to light. We need to confront the darkness and honor who she was."

As they gathered, Ruby felt a shift in the atmosphere. The collective yearning to unveil the truth ignited something magnificent in those who had come to pay homage to Emma. They stood together as a remembrance—that even in the opacity of questions, connection could provide clarity, and shadows might reveal truths hidden in the past.

Suddenly, in the distance, a figure approached. Ruby's heart skipped a beat as she squinted against the fading sunlight. It was Alex.

"Let me speak!" he called out, his voice strained but filled with commanding urgency.

The tension in the crowd escalated, whispers circulating as many took a cautious step back. Ruby felt her pulse quicken as they all turned their attention toward him.

"Alex, this isn't the time," Ruby said firmly, her heart racing. "We're here to honor Emma."

"I'm here to tell the truth," Alex shot back, desperation etched into his features. He stepped forward into the circle formed by the audience, tension crackling in the air. "You want to hear my side of what happened? You need to understand the full story—there are lies threaded in this narrative."

A low murmur swept through the crowd as Ruby met Alex's gaze, her heart pounding. "What do you mean?"

"Emma felt trapped; I can't deny it," he began, his tone shifting from defensive to earnest. "But I cared for her deeply. I was drawn into darkness myself—a darkness that distorted everything she was trying to create. That night, it all came crashing down—we were arguing about her future, about our relationship, and she just… she was so torn."

In that confrontation, Ruby felt the breath of memories dancing around her, refusing to remain hidden any longer. "But you could have done more. You could have supported her, and instead, there was a disconnect," she retorted, unable to hold back her frustration.

"You don't understand," Alex replied, pain radiating through his voice. "With Emma, everything felt like an eclipse. I was terrified of losing her, and in those moments, I failed her… I failed myself. And yes, I drove her into shadows that spiraled beyond my control."

"Did you see where she went after all this happened?" Ruby pressed, her heart steadying as she focused on the possibility of revelation in his words.

"I'm… I'm not sure about the specifics," he admitted, his facade breaking slightly. "I remember her running off after the argument. I couldn't chase her; I was overwhelmed by my feelings."

Alex paused, sorrow washing over his face. "But afterward, I heard whispers. She was seen near the river later that night… I thought she'd just left the gallery to cool off."

"But then a sense of guilt crept in afterward," he continued, a tremor edging into his voice. "I was the last person to ever see her, and when the news broke about her disappearance, all I felt was dread. She was the brightest light, and I let my shadows suffocate her."

The rawness of his expression echoed in the group, and the gravity of the moment washed over Ruby. "Do you think you can help us find out what happened next? She deserves to be honored."

There, beneath the brilliance of the setting sun and the gathering of hearts craving truth, Alex took a step forward, vulnerability washing over him like the first light breaking dawn. It felt like a crack had appeared in the darkness he and Emma shared.

"I'll help you," he said resolutely, voice steadying as he began to understand the importance of facing the shadows. "But if I do, we need to confront the memories together. There are pieces that others have yet to discover. Together, we can unfold the moments that led to that night. Only then can we honor her memory."

As Ruby met the gaze of her friends, she felt hope spark in her chest. The path they were treading was fraught with danger, and shadows loomed heavily, but the gathering of stories began to untangle the knots that obscured Emma's truth.

Maybe, just maybe, amidst the shadows they chased, they could turn pain into light and bring forward a hidden story worthy of being told. With that realization, Ruby felt a weight lift—a breakthrough had finally begun, igniting the hope that the truth would reveal itself once again.

CHAPTER 17

Lockdown

The following week unfolded with a sense of urgency as Ruby, Bella, Liv, Jace, and even Alex began to carve a path toward uncovering Emma's truth. After their intense confrontation at the park and Alex's surprising willingness to support their investigation, the group had gathered more information about Emma and the dynamics surrounding her life leading up to her disappearance.

But just as progress seemed to build momentum like a wave cresting toward the shore, unexpected news arrived like a thunderclap—a lockdown was declared across the city.

It started subtly, with a notification ringing loudly on their phones on a Wednesday afternoon. The department of public safety had issued a notice, urging residents to remain indoors due to an unfolding situation involving a recent increase in neighborhood crimes and a report of suspicious activity related to an ongoing investigation. It warned people to be cautious and avoid unnecessary travel.

"Are you kidding me?" Ruby exclaimed, staring at her phone, dread pooling in her stomach. "This can't be happening right now."

Bella, who had also just seen the alert, frowned in disbelief. "With everything we've been working on, now we're stuck inside? What about our plans to confront Alex and see deeper into that connection?"

"It's only temporary," Liv reassured, though her voice faltered slightly. "We just need to wait this out. Maybe we could use this time to dig into the information we've gathered so far."

"Staying idle isn't what we need right now," Ruby insisted, the fire in her heart flaring up. "I don't want to lose momentum. We've come too far!"

Jace nodded, glancing out the window. "But it's still a risk. If there really is danger out there, we might not want to be roaming the streets, especially if Alex was already feeling the pressures of shadows. We need a strategy to keep the information we've gathered without venturing too far."

The effortless warmth of being together in Ruby's apartment began to shift into a cocoon of restlessness and frustration. The looming storm clouds, both outside and within their hearts, began to cast a shadow over their power to act.

"Okay, let's try to brainstorm ideas without going outside. We could set up a strategy through our phones," Ruby proposed, her mind racing. "Let's compile everything we know about Emma, Alex, and any potential witnesses we had encountered before the lockdown."

The group settled into an uneasy rhythm, brainstorming late into the evening as tensions rose like the storm clouds gathering outside. They sat at Ruby's dining table, pouring over their notes, reflections, and memories that could potentially close the gap in their understanding of Emma's case.

But as the hours wore on and daylight slipped into a heavy darkness, Ruby couldn't shake the feeling that time was running out. With Alex confined to his own mysterious shadows and the communication line severed, doubt flooded her thoughts.

"What if Alex doesn't have the answers? What if we lose the opportunity to find Emma's truth altogether?" Ruby whispered, her voice laced with concern. "I can't shake this feeling that something urgent awaits us."

Just then, a loud crack vibrated through the air outside, causing them all to jump. It was shortly followed by the cacophony of sirens wailing in the distance, and the tension in Ruby's apartment immediately thickened.

"Do you think something's actually happening?" Liv asked, her eyes wide with alarm.

"I don't know," Ruby replied, her skin prickling. "But it can't be anything good."

As the sirens echoed like ominous harbingers through the neighborhood, an unsettling reality began to settle in their hearts. The sense of the world outside becoming increasingly unstable was overwhelming.

Heavy footsteps echoed in the hallway, punctuating the atmosphere thick with uncertainty. Suddenly, the doorbell rang, startling them all.

"Who could that be?" Bella asked, glancing nervously toward Ruby. "Should we answer it?"

"They might be enforcing the lockdown," Jace advised, taking a cautious step toward the door. "But we can't take risks."

"Maybe we should just wait?" Ruby suggested, anxiety lacing her voice. "Whoever it is should know we're staying inside."

However, the knocking persisted, firm and insistent, sending jitters down Ruby's spine. "We can't ignore it," she said, her instincts urging her to learn who was out there.

Taking a deep breath, Ruby approached the door cautiously, peering through the peephole. Her heart sank when she saw two uniformed officers standing outside, casting grim silhouettes in the dim light.

"Open up!" one of them called, a level tone matching the seriousness of the situation. "This is a police inquiry. We need to talk to anyone inside."

"Open the door, Ruby," Jace urged quietly, a sense of urgency tinging his tone.

With trembling hands, she unlatched the door and pulled it open slightly, allowing just enough for the officers to step inside. Both officers retained stern expressions, their eyes scanning the area for potential threats.

"Are you all alright?" one of the officers asked, his voice authoritative yet tinged with concern. "We need to make sure you're safe during the lockdown. There's been an increase in suspicious activity in the area."

"We're fine," Ruby replied shakily, trying to maintain composure. "But what's happening?"

"There's been a possible sighting of a suspect tied to a local missing person case related to Emma. We're currently advising everyone to stay indoors until we have accurate information," the officer explained, his gaze earnest and alert.

With the topic of Emma surfacing so pointedly, Ruby felt a rush of emotions flood her system, spurring her thoughts into overdrive. "Are you saying Alex might be involved?"

"We have to investigate all angles, but we can't confirm anything yet." The other officer stepped forward, his demeanor serious. "However, it's imperative that you remain vigilant. We urge you to avoid contact with anyone you suspect may be involved until we finish our inquiries. We don't want to escalate any situations."

As they surveyed the room, Ruby felt the weight of their words press down upon her, settling heavily over the collective determination in the air. "But we were just about to uncover more about Emma's past," she protested, her voice barely above a whisper. "We've been gathering stories!"

"That's important work," the first officer acknowledged, holding her gaze sincerely. "But the priority right now is ensuring your safety. We're asking everyone to comply with the lockdown until we've gathered the necessary information."

With the officers cautiously departing, Ruby felt the room grow colder, shadows creeping in and tightening around them. They were all caught in a nebulous moment of uncertainty, the very progress they had made now seeming precarious.

"What do we do now?" Liv asked, her voice quivering slightly. "We can't just sit here."

Ruby's heart raced as she struggled to grasp the reality of the situation. "We have to stay alert. We can't let this turmoil intimidate us. We need to keep our notes, connections, and plans organized in a way that allows us to move when the time is right," she asserted, feeling the embers of resolve stirring within her.

As the hours passed, a heavy stillness enveloped the apartment, and the lockdown created a cocoon, holding the team captive but also allowing for reflection and reprieve from the chaos unfolding outside.

In that tension-filled silence, they reviewed the threads of Emma's story once more—the whispers, the fears, the emotional connections that had propelled them forward into this investigation. Finding solace in the potential that sprang from uncertainty became their shared mission.

And as uncertainty wrapped tighter around them, finally, a thought broke through the tension: Sometimes, shadows whisper secrets waiting to be unveiled.

As the eerie sounds of sirens faded into the distance, Ruby vowed to uncover the truths hidden in the intertwining darkness, convinced that they would not only chase shadows but emerge with powerful revelations—ones that would lead them to Emma, and perhaps even bring closure to the haunting echoes of the past.

Chapter 18

Beyond the Frame

The lockdown extended through the night, turning Ruby's apartment into a sanctuary filled with both disquiet and resolve. Shadows lingered around them as they continued to pore over Emma's art, notes, and the recent revelations about her involvement with Alex. Ruby felt an amalgam of emotions swirling within her — fear, determination, and a lingering sorrow for the light that Emma had embodied.

After hours of collective reflection, Ruby finally spoke up, breaking the silence. "We need to find a way to push past these confines. The lockdown may keep us within physical limits, but we still have tools at our disposal."

"What are you thinking?" Bella asked, her eyes alert, bright with hope.

"While we're trapped here, let's explore everything we have — every document, every photograph. Maybe we can uncover insights that lead us closer to Emma's narrative," Ruby suggested, grasping the idea of using their time wisely.

"Good thinking. We can explore the context of her artwork beyond just the visible," Jace concurred as he sorted through the collection of Emma's sketches they had brought along.

Energized by Ruby's breakthrough, the quartet dove back into their research, spreading the art pieces and notes across the living room floor in an organized chaos. Under the twinkling light of Ruby's string lights, they began connecting dots that had evaded them before.

"Look at this," Ruby said as she placed her finger on one of Emma's drawings, a delicate interpretation of a woman standing at the edge of a river, gazing into the depths. "The river — it represents so much: a journey, emotions flowing, a bridge to the unknown. I think it's more than just a metaphor," she explained, excitement building in her voice.

"So, you're saying this artwork ties back to Emma's feelings?" Liv asked, her eyes lighting up. "Maybe the river symbolizes her struggle to navigate her emotions — a place where shadowy figures might creep in."

"Exactly!" Ruby replied, feeling the energy of collaboration surge through them. "And Alex was one of those shadows. We need to analyze every aspect of Emma's life as she portrayed it in her art."

Bella chimed in, her excitement bubbling over. "If Emma used symbolism in her artwork, perhaps it isn't merely personal. Maybe she intended to convey broader themes about her struggles. Those themes might resonate with others who are facing their depths or obligations just as she was."

"That's worth exploring further!" Jace agreed. "Let's break this down. We can identify patterns and figure out what Emma was encapsulating beyond just the visuals."

Ruby looked around at the vibrant artworks, the stories woven into each piece coming to life as they discussed them. "We have this unique collection of her creative expression; let's utilize it to find those connections, not just within her circle, but outside of it too. Maybe we can even contact others from this gathering to get their perspectives."

As the hours passed, Ruby and her friends meticulously connected themes in Emma's work to the emotional struggles and relationships that had defined her journey. They dissected the river motif — each twist and turn signifying struggles woven with the joys of connection.

Then, Ruby's gaze fell upon a folded sketch hidden beneath a stack of photographs. As she unfolded it, her breath hitched —a drawing of a bridge over a winding river, surrounded by twinkling lights swinging gently in the night sky.

"This is beautiful!" Ruby breathed, her heart racing. "Emma portrayed the bridge as if it were both a journey and a barrier. This could definitely represent her relationship with Alex: the connection of two worlds with underlying struggles."

"What else does it say?" Bella leaned in, an eagerness brightening her eyes.

On the bottom edge, Ruby spotted a scribbled note that read: "All paths lead somewhere; some to places of light, others to darkness. I just have to find my way back to the bridge."

"That implies her yearning for connection," Liv noted quietly. "Perhaps her struggle wasn't just with Alex, but with her own place in the world. She felt lost."

Ruby nodded, a wave of realization washing over her. "This was Emma trying to reach for clarity while wrestling with her emotional turmoil. It's incredible how much she embedded into her art."

"Indeed," Jace agreed, his voice a murmur filled with awe. "Emma's art not only reflected personal struggles but also intertwined narratives—her own shadows combining with those of others around her. This could unlock more than just her story!"

As they continued discussing their findings, Ruby felt a simmering energy in the air. They were picking apart the dimensions of Emma's life, contextualizing unspoken connections that spanned from Emma to her family, friends, and ultimately to Alex. Each revelation felt like stepping further into Emma's memories, uncovering layers that had long been buried under darkness.

Suddenly, Bella interrupted their conversation with a sudden query. "What if Emma wrote about her art in some capacity? Did she keep notes about her pieces?"

"I'll search through the papers," Ruby said, flipping through Emma's accumulated sketches and notes to find context. As she rifled through the pile, she gasped when she found a stack of old poems alongside the drawings — poems that reflected her struggles and dreams. Each verse wielded raw emotion, capturing Emma's essence like the brushstrokes on her canvases.

"Look at this one," Ruby began to read aloud, her voice steady but filled with reverence. "In the river's depths, I groom my heart; the shadows dance, but I play my part. Each swirl and eddy—my emotions collide, yet the glimmer of hope I'll not let slide."

The resonance of the poem hung in the air like a fragile lantern illuminating their purpose. "She even created connections with the river in her poetry—each line draped in meaning," Ruby said, feeling the energy intensify around them.

"That speaks to her feelings about the conflict in her life, doesn't it?" Jace asked, rapt by the way Ruby's words reverberated through the room. "It's like she understood the balance she needed to achieve but felt torn."

"And it could outline her thoughts about her relationship with Alex even more," Liv pointed out, a tremor in her voice as she sensed their progress.

With every poem they uncovered, with every emotional connection they navigated, the walls of uncertainty began to dissolve. It felt as though each revelation brought them one step closer to finding the heart of Emma's struggle, the shadows receding as if chased away by the light of understanding.

As they delved deeper, they realized they had effectively constructed their own bridge—a bridge leading back to Emma, connecting her legacy to their present pursuit.

"Should we start compiling these pieces into something larger? A tribute?" Bella asked, her eyes shining with resolve.

"Yes," Ruby said, her heart soaring with hope. "A tribute to honor Emma's memory and reveal the complexities of her life. We can combine her art, poetry, and stories into a cohesive narrative that integrates various perspectives that shape who she was."

As they began sorting through the sketches and notes, Ruby felt a firm belief grow within her: they would reclaim Emma's narrative and bring the light back to the shadows—never allowing her story to fade beneath time and silence.

With a deep sense of conviction, they decided that the gathering at the park was no longer just about remembrance; it would be a celebration and a pursuit of the truth they sought. Through every piece of Emma's artistry, they would ensure her legacy echoed loud and clear amid all those who had loved her, illuminating the hidden truths that had long remained undiscovered.

As the last rays of light dipped below the horizon, Ruby felt invigorated by the possibilities stretching ahead. In chasing shadows, perhaps they could finally bring Emma into the light.

CHAPTER 19

Confronting the Past

Dawn crept across the horizon like a whisper, bringing the promise of a new day. The anticipation hung heavy in Ruby's apartment as she prepared for the gathering in the park. Emma's story had brought them to this critical moment, a convergence of emotions, memories, and unresolved truths begging to be unveiled.

After days of deep reflection and laboring through Emma's artwork and poetry, Ruby had rallied her friends around a singular purpose: it was time to confront the heart of Emma's narrative, including Alex, and unveil the shadows that lingered over her life once and for all.

As the phone buzzed with notifications, Ruby's heart raced. The gathering was set to begin shortly, and the air once again buzzed with anticipation. She glanced around at the display they had arranged—vibrant photographs, sketches, and printed poems—including the collage they had unearthed from Emma's belongings. Each piece served as a portal into her world, inviting those gathered to share their stories and memories of the artist who had sparked inspiration and reflection in everyone who had known her.

"Are you ready?" Bella asked, adjusting the centerpiece—a beautiful bouquet of wildflowers at the center of their makeshift display.

"Ready as I'll ever be," Ruby said, though her voice trembled slightly, betraying the flurry of emotions brewing within.

"We've got this," Liv reassured, placing her hand on Ruby's shoulder. "The most important thing is honoring Emma and creating a safe space for everyone to share their experiences."

As they made their way to the park, the spring air felt fresh and alive, infused with the spirit of possibility. The sun shone brightly above, a reminder of radiant moments that Emma had captured through her art.

Upon arriving at the park, they were greeted by a small crowd gathered under the large oak tree, where they had set up their display. Familiar faces mingled with new ones, each one reflecting a connection to Emma — friends, acquaintances, and even a few art enthusiasts who had been inspired by her pieces. Ruby felt a flutter of hope rise inside her; it was as if Emma's spirit was shining through these connections.

"Looks like we have a good turnout!" Jace remarked, walking alongside Ruby and Liv as they approached the group.

"Yeah!" Bella said, beaming with excitement. "This is more than I could have imagined. People genuinely want to honor her memory!"

As they set up their display, Ruby felt the tension transform into collective energy, as everyone mingled and began to share stories about Emma. Participants occasionally stepped forward to recite pieces of poetry, tales of laughter, and heartfelt reflections on the meaningful impact she had on their lives.

After amorphous but graceful conversations circulated for a while, Ruby cleared her throat, stepping in front of the group to offer some words of introduction. "Thank you all for coming today. We gather not just to remember Emma but to bring forward her story amid the shadows that threaten to drown her legacy. We aim to realize her light, her creativity, and the profound impact she had on those around her."

A hush fell over the crowd, and Ruby's heart raced as she continued. "Each of you carries an element of Emma's spirit with you, whether you knew her as a friend, a fellow artist, or a member of this community. A few days ago, we began to confront disappearing shadows while collecting stories of her life. Today, we want to keep that momentum going."

As Ruby turned and gestured toward the vibrant display, she felt a wave of strength wash over her. "We also have Alex here with us," she said with conviction, glancing toward the figure who had quietly emerged from the fringe of the gathering. "He's part of Emma's story, and we believe in confronting the questions surrounding their relationship as we honor her memory."

The crowd murmured, their interest piqued. Alex stood beside Ruby, shadows faintly clinging to his figure, but as he prepared to speak, a ripple of uncertainty ran through the gathering.

"I know that my presence may bring discomfort. I wasn't always the friend Emma needed," Alex began hesitantly, his voice shaky yet steadying. "But I'm here to confront my own past, to honor the light Emma brought into the world, and to bring forth the shadows that haunt us all."

Ruby's heart leaped as she felt the air crackle with the weight of Alex's admission. "Thank you for being here, Alex. We're deeply committed to bringing Emma's truth to light," she responded, her gaze locking with his.

As Alex continued, he began to unravel deeper insights about his relationship with Emma, his emotions spilling over each word he spoke. "I let my envy and darkness cloud my judgment, and Emma became a target for my shadows. She always possessed a unique light—a radiance that attracted people—yet I allowed my insecurities to drive her away," he admitted, vulnerability enveloping his voice.

His words echoed in the hearts of everyone gathered. Some murmured in quiet shock, while others listened intently, feeling the weight of the honesty permeating the atmosphere.

"We want to know more," Ruby encouraged gently. "What were Emma's last days like? Did you witness anything that makes sense of her disappearance?"

"She fought against the darkness as best she could," Alex continued, glancing at the crowd with sincerity spilling from his gaze. "But the connection we shared became a storm. And that night… there was an argument, yes, but I was worried I was about to lose everything. Shadows intertwine, but her light began to flicker; I pushed her away, and ultimately, it hurt both of us."

The group paused, allowing the weight of his confession to seep in, filling the air with a palpable tension. Ruby allowed silence to stretch for a moment, letting the gathered reflections wash over the crowd.

Then, someone in the back shouted, "But we need to know what happened to her after that! Did you see where she went, Alex? Did she mention anything?"

The intensity of the moment reached a fever pitch, as Alex's face tightened with uncertainty. "I don't know exactly what happened after the argument, but I remember Emma speaking about needing to find clarity near the river," he revealed, his voice low but charged with emotion. "I thought she would return home, but in my mind, those shadows suffocated the possibility of her doing so."

The murmurs in the crowd deepened, building a sense of urgency to piece together Emma's story. Ruby felt a swell of hope mixed with sorrow as the threads of their conversations began to weave back together, joining the memories they had all gathered.

In the coming moments, stories began to pour out from various members of the gathering. Patrons sharing snippets of memories they held, echoing sentiments of Emma carrying brilliance even when navigating the shadows that choked at her spirit.

And as time passed, a new wave of clarity began to form over the gathering. Memories collected turned into a powerful tapestry, revealing that Emma had fought valiantly against the struggles that shadowed her life for as long as she could. Pieces of her spirit began to rise from within the community as everyone shared their light—stories filled with laughter and creativity, collectively reclaiming her essence.

As Ruby stood at the center of all that love, she felt both humbled and empowered. Each story surged through her, transforming what had begun as a search for answers into a beautiful celebration of Emma's legacy.

"Thank you all for sharing these moments," Ruby finally spoke, her voice filled with gratitude. "It's in sharing that we weave together the fabric of Emma's life—her artistry, her light, and her struggles. We must remember that while shadows may linger, they never erase her brilliance. It's by bringing these memories back into the light that we embrace the spirit of who Emma was. She deserves that, and so do we."

As the gathering continued, Ruby could see the constellation of stories intertwining—a reminder that within the shadows, there always existed the possibility of light. The distance between pain and healing shrank as they all shared their truths, forging connections that transcended darkness.

In that moment, Ruby felt she was chasing shadows for the right reasons: to embrace the intricacies of Emma's life and honor her journey as they brought the light forth against the dusk of uncertainty.

CHAPTER 20

The Photos Tell the Tale

As the sun began setting on the horizon, the park transformed into a canvas painted in warm hues of orange and pink. Ruby stood surrounded by her friends and those who had come to remember Emma, her heart swelling with both sadness and hope. The gathering had become more than just a tribute; it was a testament to the connections forged through the stories shared and the memories awakened.

After an hour of stories, laughter, and tears, Ruby felt a surge of inspiration wash over her. The importance of visuals became apparent as memories echoed through the air like strands of music woven together. Emma's artwork had touched countless lives, and it occurred to Ruby that they had the opportunity to capture that essence through the photographs they had taken. The photographs served as a bridge between the past and the present, illustrating the impact Emma had left on those gathered.

"Let's do something special with the photos we've captured today," Ruby proposed, gathering her friends and the attendees together. "We can create a visual story about Emma's life using these images, along with the memories you've shared. We can combine this with her art to honor who she was."

"That's perfect," Bella said enthusiastically, her excitement bubbling. "We can set up a scrapbook of sorts, blending the essence of Emma's life with both stories and visuals that portray her spirit."

Liv chimed in, "We can use quotes from Emma's poetry and snippets of her art alongside the photographs and reflections from today. It can be a way to honor her legacy while preserving the memories shared in this gathering."

"Exactly!" Ruby replied, her heart racing at the prospect. "Let's make this a living tribute, something that embodies Emma's light and the connections she built."

With renewed purpose, they set to work, gathering photographs, sketches, and quotes, creating a mosaic of Emma's life. Attendees contributed their own photos if they had them—some shared images from concerts Emma went to, others brought out videos they had captured during their time together. Each piece added depth to the collage they were creating.

As they worked, Ruby became even more aware of the emotional threads binding them together. The joy in their shared laughter contrasted sharply with a current of sadness that occasionally swept through, reminding everyone of the light that had been lost. But it also felt oddly cathartic, like they were collectively breathing life back into Emma's spirit.

They gathered by the picnic tables where their tribute was coming to fruition, and Ruby asked everyone to share their reflections more verbally. The phones and cameras filled with images, and soon enough, the table overflowed with the stories etched on glossy paper, faces beaming with joy and nostalgia.

"Here's one of Emma at that concert—such a delight!" one of the attendees said, passing a printed photograph. "She loved music; it always inspired her art."

"I think this captures her zest for life perfectly," Ruby said, placing it alongside an illustration Emma had drawn during a music festival.

Another participant shared an old photo of Emma at the park, sketching under the oak tree where they were gathered. "She used to sit here for hours, lost in her world, capturing moments."

"That sums up who she was—a beautiful tapestry of experiences and emotions," Liv remarked, her eyes glinting with tears yet shining with light.

As they began to create a central display, Ruby's mind drifted to Alex's earlier words. He had acknowledged that shadows often intermingled with light, and she felt a longing to merge both elements into this tribute. After all, the narrative they were piecing together was not just about Emma's struggles but also about celebrating her brilliance.

After a few hours of dedication, their tribute gradually took shape — a vibrant collage of Emma's spirit encompassing photographs, notes, artwork, and heartfelt messages from those who loved her, mingling with the shared stories and laughter.

Once everything was set, Ruby stepped back and surveyed the creation before them. It was more than just a compilation of memories; it was an emotional journey that reflected Emma's essence and the depth of lives she had touched.

"Does everyone want to share what Emma means to you?" Ruby proposed, her heart racing as she sensed the importance of voices coming together to celebrate her legacy.

One by one, attendees began to step forward, sharing their stories of how Emma had touched their lives—how her unwavering spirit had inspired them, how her laughter had brightened their darkest days, how her art had given them hope. With each speaker, Ruby's heart expanded, feeling both grief and gratitude swirl within her.

"I met Emma during a painting class; she urged me to explore my creativity," one woman shared, wiping a tear from her cheek. "I would've never pursued it without her encouragement."

Another added, "I didn't realize how much I was missing until I experienced Emma's genuine kindness. She was always there, always listening, ready to uplift everyone around her."

As the emotional tributes unfolded, Ruby felt them wrap around her, enveloping her with warmth and sorrow alike. It was both cathartic and bittersweet, reminding everyone present of their shared humanity—the joys and sorrows that intertwined like colors on a canvas.

"What I loved most about Emma was her ability to turn pain into beauty," Jace said, stepping forward. "Her art was a reflection of the light and darkness within her, and that very attitude touched us all."

At this moment, Ruby felt the energy of the crowd shift, as if an invisible bond tethered them together, creating a warm safety net around their emotions.

Then she felt a gentle nudge in her heart. "I think it's time to honor Emma through an act of remembrance. Let's finish this tribute by lighting candles in her honor," she suggested, her voice steadying as she looked around the gathering.

One of the participants stepped forward, bringing forth a box filled with small candles, their flickering light promising to illuminate the collective spirit emanating from everyone present. Ruby guided everyone in a brief moment of stillness as they ignited each candle, allowing the flames to flicker and dance in the soft evening breeze—each one representing not just Emma's life but also the paths they would all continue to walk.

As the last candle was lit, Ruby took a moment before speaking, her heart swelling with emotion. "Tonight, we come together to celebrate Emma's life, her light, and the legacy she left behind. In sharing our stories, we reconnect with Emma's spirit and foster connections that bridge the gaps—those between the light, the art, the shadow, and our own lives."

In that moment, the air shimmered with the shared reverence, each candle standing as a beacon against the encroaching darkness and a reminder of the love they held for Emma.

The gathering became a beautiful reflection of hope, a testament that love and art have the power to transcend loss, weaving together the memories of those they hold dear. The photos, the stories, and the flames flickering brightly against the dusk all served to remind them that even amidst shadows, light can always find a way to break through.

As the night continued, Ruby knew their mission had shifted from merely uncovering Emma's truth to embracing the fullness of who she was. They would honor her memory, cherish her legacy, and let the light of her spirit continue to shine brightly in their lives.

With Emma's story unfolding before their eyes, Ruby felt buoyed by the realization that while they would continue to chase shadows, the light they carried together would guide them every step of the way.

CHAPTER 21

Twists and Turns

The days following the gathering felt surreal, as if Ruby and her friends were emerging from a vivid dream into a world altered by the revelations they had shared. The candles that flickered in remembrance of Emma had illuminated not just her spirit, but also ignited a deeper determination among the group to uncover the intricacies of her life. Yet the clouds of uncertainty still loomed overhead, their promise of resolutions stretching into the unknown.

In Ruby's apartment, the air buzzed with anticipation. Their walls were adorned with images and notes gathered during their investigation, a patchwork of Emma's life and the people she had touched. Each artifact told a story — they were glimpses into a journey shrouded in complexity, and now, they found themselves standing at the edge of new revelations.

"Alright, team, it's time to compile everything we've learned so far," Ruby said, glancing around at the spread of photographs, journal entries, and the ever-growing list of people they needed to follow up with. "We need a game plan moving forward."

Jace nodded, his eyes scanning the notes. "We've got some solid leads that touch on both Emma's relationships and her struggles with Alex. But we need to reach out to a few more individuals who can help fill in the gaps. There's a growing sense that there are people who still have stories to tell—

perhaps even people related to Alex who saw things go wrong."

"Let's start with that," Bella chimed in. "We need to compile an updated list of everyone we've spoken to and who we should reach out to next."

Liv pulled out a notebook she had been using to keep track of their contacts. "I've already jotted down names based on our discussions and the gathering. We should focus on reaching out to any friends or colleagues of Emma who can provide insight into her emotional state leading up to her disappearance."

As they reviewed their list, Ruby's mind wandered toward Alex. Part of her felt sympathy for him, understanding the weight of his own struggles; yet another part couldn't shake the uneasy sense of responsibility that came with his involvement in Emma's life. Should they confront him again, or steer clear for the time being?

With the decisions made and their spirits raised, Ruby decided they would conduct their exploration with caution. They spent hours making calls, sending messages, and setting up meetings with potential witnesses — each connection weaving a tighter web of inquiry around Emma's last days. The sense of urgency grew with each possible lead they gathered, thickening in the air between them.

Within a few days, the universe responded, leading them to a local artist who had once collaborated with Emma. His name was Noah, and he had agreed to meet them at a cozy café nearby.

When they arrived at the café, Ruby felt a mixture of excitement and nerves coursing through her veins. This was another opportunity to dig through the layers and shadowy complexity of Emma's life.

"Let's keep everything focused on Emma and not on Alex yet," Jace suggested as they settled around a small table under a window adorned with flowing ivy. "We want to hear what Noah has to say about her work and emotional state."

Ruby nodded, her heart racing at the impending conversation. Moments later, a tall man with tousled brown hair and a laid-back demeanor approached their table. "Hey there! You must be Ruby, Bella, Liv, and Jace," he said, a genuine smile lighting up his face. "Thanks for inviting me to join. I hear you've been on quite the quest concerning Emma."

"Glad to meet you, Noah," Ruby replied, her excitement building. "We've been gathering memories and insights into Emma's life, especially around the time before she vanished. You collaborated with her; we were hoping to gain some more perspective on her emotional state during that period."

"Of course," Noah said, settling into his seat with an air of earnestness. "Emma was a remarkable artist. Her work always encapsulated so many layers, but I could tell she was grappling with a lot beneath the surface."

"What do you mean by that?" Bella asked, leaning in to listen intently.

"Well, we collaborated on a few pieces, but toward the end of our partnership, I sensed she was pulling away," Noah explained, hesitating as if choosing his words carefully. "She wanted to explore certain themes more deeply, like those shadows she hinted at in her art. It was both beautiful and haunting."

"The struggle between light and darkness?" Ruby interjected, feeling the pieces of their investigation align.

"No doubt," Noah replied, his gaze distant as he reflected on their partnership. "There were hints of internal conflict — I saw her grappling with expectations versus the authenticity of her work. But despite my efforts to connect, she withdrew. It felt like a storm brewing beneath the surface."

"Have you ever spoken to Alex during that time?" Jace asked, eager to connect more dots.

Noah frowned slightly as he considered the question. "Yes, he was occasionally around. Emma spoke about him like he was someone she was wrestling against, but I couldn't pinpoint the extent of their relationship. He had this intense energy, and I could see how it affected Emma."

This ignited a spark of determination within Ruby. "Did you witness their relationship change the way Emma approached her art? Was there a specific moment when you knew he was impacting her negatively?"

"I remember it well," Noah said, shifting his gaze. "We were preparing for an exhibition together when I sensed she was confused. The way she looked at her own work was different —haunted. There was something about that night. I noticed Alex lurking in the shadows, and the atmosphere shifted; it ended up being a tipping point for her."

"What happened?" Bella pressed, her tone insistent.

"We had a late-night discussion—Emma had planned to unveil a piece revolving around freedom and self-identity," Noah recalled. "She seemed restless, a mix of fear and excitement, but then she had an argument with Alex. The tension escalated, and the energy shifted once he entered the gallery. I watched as she began to fade, and I could only stand back silently wishing to intervene."

Ruby felt the air grow heavy with the implied truths. "Is there any way we could reach out to him? If Alex became a negative figure in Emma's life, we might be able to confront the source of her pain," she suggested.

"Honestly, I think that's risky," Noah cautioned, concern all over his face. "If you approach him, he might close up. He's unpredictable. I think channeling Emma's spirit through her work is the best course — her art speaks louder than anything else. Maybe uncovering more of her visual language will lead you to the deeper narratives."

Determined, Ruby took a breath. "I agree; delving deeper into Emma's artistic vision can pave the way to whatever truth has yet to emerge. But it's a different kind of confrontation; one focused on her message instead of Alex's shadows."

As they continued to talk, they gathered more names of acquaintances Emma had known over the years and promised Noah to dig deeper into Emma's art. They discussed the importance of honoring her memory as they sought greater understanding and uncovering more connections.

By the end of their conversation, Ruby felt a wave of gratitude for Noah's insights. They had managed to uncover more threads about Emma's life, revealing layers of meaning hidden behind each work of art. The weight of sorrow had lessened slightly, replaced by the hope that they could celebrate Emma through her legacy.

As they said their goodbyes and stepped back into the bustling city, Ruby felt ready to confront whatever shadows persisted. "The more we gather, the clearer the picture becomes," she said, her determination sharp.

But just as they were about to part ways, a voice in the distance caught Ruby's attention. "Ruby!"

She turned to find a familiar face — it was Eva from the café, rushing toward them, her expression frantic.

"I've been trying to chase you down!" she exclaimed, breathless. "There was a police bulletin I saw — they're investigating something related to Emma's case. A potential sighting of a stranger they believe might have influenced her disappearance."

Ruby's heart raced, anticipation swelling within her as the significance of Eva's words settled in. "What do you mean? A sighting of who?"

Eva slowed her breathing, the weight of her message pressing heavily on everyone's shoulders. "They're questioning people in the area about Alex. They believe he could have been involved deeper than anyone realized."

"Are they also discussing the appearance of someone else?" Jace interjected, his eyes widening in realization. "Someone who was a common thread among those witnessing Emma's final days?"

"Exactly," Eva replied, catching her breath. "We need to move quickly. They said if anyone has leads or memories to share, they should come forward. We may have a chance to uncover the truth if we put the pieces together before the authorities close the case for good."

The urgency of the moment washed over Ruby as adrenaline surged within her veins. "We can't waste time—we need to gather everyone and share as much as we can before it's too late. It'll be our chance to confront the past once and for all."

As they mobilized to follow this new lead, the shadows that had once threatened their journey now felt different, crackling with anticipation. Perhaps the answers they sought were finally within their grasp. And perhaps the truth about Emma's disappearance loomed closer than ever — just beyond the frame of her life's artwork, ready to reveal itself in the light they had long fought to uncover.

CHAPTER 22

The Last Clue

The atmosphere in Ruby's apartment was charged with anticipation as the group prepared for what could be a pivotal moment in their investigation into Emma's disappearance. Local authorities had issued alerts mentioning a possible sighting of Alex, urging anyone with information to share it. Ruby felt a mix of exhilaration and anxiety; they were racing against time to gather what they could before the case grew cold once more.

"Alright, everyone's pouring in for the meeting, but we still have time to review our notes," Ruby said, glancing at the notes scattered across the living room table. The sunlight streaming through the window fueled her determination. "We need to make sure we're organized and ready to share everything we know, especially about Alex and Emma's interactions."

"I went back to Emma's sketches and journal entries again," Bella said as she flipped through the pages of Emma's poetry and reflections that had become a backbone of their investigation. "I think there's a connection worth examining even more closely. Her references to the river could symbolize her emotional current — a theme that represents both conflict and resolution."

"If the river's currents imply a deeper complexity in her feelings," Liv added quickly, "then this could tie into the last few hours before she vanished. We might connect the dots we've missed."

Jace scoured the surface of their notes, piecing together quotes and revelations. "We need to remember that we're searching for shadows — the double meanings that could evoke new perspectives. If we rethink the river not just as a getaway but also as a confronting force, we might uncover Emma's disposition leading to that final confrontation."

Ruby nodded in agreement, feeling the pulse of possibilities filling the air. As they exchanged ideas and intertwined stories, the room filled with a sense of camaraderie and resolve—a commitment to unveiling Emma's journey.

Just then, the door swung open, and attendees from their previous gathering began to filter into the apartment. Familiar faces filled the space, each person carrying stories and emotions ripe for sharing. Ruby felt the warmth of connection and purpose envelop her; everyone present was united in their quest to honor Emma's life and seek the truth that had eluded them for so long.

"Thank you all for making it," Ruby said, stepping forward to address the gathering. "As you know, we're here to uncover the details surrounding Emma's disappearance, and the authorities are urging everyone to come forward with any pieces of information they may have regarding Alex or the night of her last exhibition."

The group murmured in agreement, eager to share their own reflections and experiences over the past few days. Conversations sprang up all around, each person exchanging their takes on Emma's artistry and the profound impact she had on their lives.

Among the attendees, a stout man with a gentle beard raised his hand, catching Ruby's attention. "I have something," he said, his voice deep. "I was at that gallery opening. I may not have noticed everything, but I saw something that night that left a lasting impression."

Ruby's heart raced with anticipation. "Please, go on."

"I remember walking into the gallery when I overheard raised voices coming from behind the installation," he continued. "I thought it was just the excitement of the evening, but when I looked over, I saw Emma and Alex. He was pacing, his face flushed with anger, while Emma stood with her arms crossed, looking defensive."

"What were they arguing about?" Belle inquired, leaning forward in her seat, eagerly anticipating the unfolding moment.

"I couldn't catch every word, but I remember Emma's expression — it was a blend of defiance and sorrow. I heard her mention something about 'letting go' and 'not being defined by him.' It struck me — she was wrestling with something significant," the man recalled, his brow furrowed in worry.

"That's a strong indication she felt trapped," Ruby murmured, the pieces of the puzzle feeling more impactful. "Do you recall exactly when this happened?"

He thought for a moment. "Yes, it was right before the main crowd filtered in, just after I saw Emma chatting with others. They seemed expansive and bright, and everything shifted when Alex entered her space."

"Knowing that they argued shortly before the crowd could change everything!" Liv exclaimed, her breathing quickening

159

with excitement. "It points to a conflict that escalated within a tight timeline that night."

Ruby felt another surge of connection course through her as if the threads of their investigation were weaving themselves tighter together, illuminating an impending resolution. "This means we can contact the authorities and let them know you were there when this happened. Your witness could be incredibly significant in shedding light on Emma's and Alex's exchange."

As the room buzzed with new possibilities, someone else offered more information. "I remember seeing Emma walk toward the exit after the argument," a young woman said, her voice filled with uncertainty. "There was a moment when she glanced back, like she wanted to return, but then she left."

"Did you see where she went after she left?" Ruby asked, her heart racing with anticipation.

"I didn't, but I recall feeling unsettled after witnessing that exchange, like something wasn't right. I saw Alex clenching his fists, and I had the sense that he had crossed a line," she said, her voice catching.

The tension in the room thickened, anticipation wrapping around Ruby like a cloak. This information pointed to the possibility that Emma's world had shifted — she had felt the conflict grow and likely made the choice to step away from something heavy.

"Maybe... she left to regain her courage," Ruby contemplated aloud, piecing thoughts together like an artist assembling a canvas. "But if we consider there was a confrontation happening, could it be that she felt desperate, even as she sought clarity? The conflict likely gave rise to her need to escape."

Several attendees nodded, eyes wide with realization. Together, they pieced together the narrative, sketching the layers of emotion embedded in the shadows of the gallery. It felt like an invisible thread tied them all to Emma, a connection pulsing with vitality and pain that offered the hope for closure, not just for them, but for Emma's family too.

As they continued discussing the revelations emerging from Emma's last days, the atmosphere shifted yet again, a new energy building. Ruby felt on the edge of something profound, as if the pieces were aligning for an emotional breakthrough.

"Let's take a moment to breathe," Ruby suggested, her senses tingling with anticipation. "This is a lot to unpack, and we need to reflect on what we've collected so far. It's imperative not only to share information but also to honor Emma's journey in the process."

As everyone settled, taking a few moments to gather themselves, Ruby felt the gravity of what they were chasing seal the air around them. They weren't just seeking answers; they were rewriting the fabric of Emma's legacy—integrating memories that were more vibrant than the shadows cast over her life.

Inspired, Ruby gathered her thoughts and addressed the group again. "In every twist and turn we've taken in this investigation, we've sought to bring forth the truth. Whatever remains hidden might still hold the key to restoring Emma's light."

An unspoken resolve resonated within the crowd, the flicker of hope igniting new determination to seek the truth no matter what.

"I think we're nearing a conclusion, but every last clue brings us closer," Jace said, his tone steady. "We'll need to gather everything we've collected, reassess our leads, and determine our next course of action. It's time for everyone to embrace vulnerability, share the stories that are maybe too difficult, and allow ourselves to face the shadows that have haunted us."

With that, they began recounting their experiences, the intertwining of shadows and light more vivid than ever. Together, they chased the echoes of Emma's laughter, weaving the undeniable brilliance of her spirit into an elaborate tapestry that honored her memories.

And as the night lengthened and the stars shone overhead, Ruby felt a profound sense of connection within the community gathered. They would unveil the truth behind Emma's story and face the darkness head-on — hand in hand. Through every twist and turn of their journey, they would illuminate the way, ensuring her light would never be extinguished.

CHAPTER 23

The Showdown

The air was thick with tension as Ruby, Bella, Liv, Jace, and Alex stood together outside the old warehouse on Willow Street, the ominous building looming before them like a dark promise. After gathering memories, insights, and evidence surrounding Emma's disappearance, they felt the weight of shadowy secrets lurking just beyond reach.

Tonight, following their emotional revelations and the mounting urgency to confront Alex about Emma, they had decided it was time to face whatever darkness lingered within those walls—a premature confrontation with the past they had all been chasing.

"Are we really ready for this?" Liv asked nervously, glancing between her friends and the entrance to the warehouse. Despite her determination, Ruby could see the flicker of doubt in her eyes.

"Yes," Ruby said, feeling the strength build in her heart. "This is the moment we've been preparing for. We need to know the truth about Emma's last connection to Alex and understand how intertwining shadows may have shaped her narrative."

With a collective gulp, they stepped across the threshold, the sound of creaking wood and the smell of dampness wrapping around them like a thick fog. The interior was dimly lit, shadows dancing in the corners and reflecting the paintings that adorned the walls but felt abandoned. Flickering overhead lights created an almost surreal ambiance.

"Stay close," Jace whispered, his voice carrying the weight of caution. They moved deeper into the space, where the echoes of their footsteps reverberated against the walls, creating an unsettling harmony.

"Alex, are you sure this is where he might be?" Bella asked, her eyes scanning the room as they continued forward, each corner brimming with uncertainty.

"He could be surrounded by his crowd of artists or lurking in the deep corners," Alex replied, his voice steady yet tinged with an edge. "He often comes here to brood over his work. We need to move before questions grow louder."

As they reached the heart of the warehouse, the group spotted a figure hunched over at a table—its surface cluttered with canvases, paints, and scattered sketches. With a mixture of hope and trepidation, they ventured closer, Ruby's heart racing as she recognized the man: it was him—Alex's friend, the one often seen in the periphery of their investigation.

"Excuse me…" Ruby called out gently, drawing the man's attention. "Are you Alex? We've been looking for you."

The man looked up slowly, revealing an unkempt appearance and shadows etched into his features. "Yeah… I'm Alex." His tone was guarded, shifting effortlessly from indifference to skepticism. "What do you want?"

"We came to talk about Emma," Ruby replied, her voice steady, though nerves fluttered in her stomach. "Things have changed. You need to help us unravel what happened last time she was here. We've got questions that require answers."

"Why should I even bother?" Alex sneered, the edge of resentment mingling with a hint of sorrow. "The past is riddled with shadows, and you'll not find clarity here. What makes you think you're entitled to press me for information?"

"Because we deserve to honor her memory," Jace stepped forward, his voice firm. "It's about time someone sheds light on what happened. Your silence could make you complicit in whatever shadows chased her away."

A flicker crossed Alex's face, and for an instant, Ruby thought he might soften. Instead, he shook his head, anger spilling forth. "You don't understand! None of you do! Emma wasn't just some canvas to be analyzed. She was alive, struggling, and the whispers of her past haunt me just as much as they haunt you. The shadows followed her, and I..." His voice trailed off, and he turned away bitterly.

Ruby could feel the vulnerability embedded in his words, but she refused to relent. "You became part of those shadows," she pressed, her voice calm yet unwavering. "And it's your chance to own up to that. Did you ever confront her about her fears? What was it that made you feel threatened when you saw her with other friends? Did you ever see her around the river after that night?"

Flashes of uncertainty danced in Alex's eyes. "I... I wanted to believe I was someone special to her, but I saw her light growing apart from me—becoming warmer with others—unreachable. It terrified me... but I didn't know how to communicate that fear."

As Ruby challenged him with her gaze, he slowly lifted his eyes to meet hers. "She was looking for escape, an outlet from the burden she felt heavy on her shoulders."

Pain rippled through Ruby as realization dawned. "You thought you were losing her, but instead of being honest and facing that fear, you let it control you."

"Every moment I wasted kept me locked in shadows," Alex replied, anguish spilling from his voice. "And so Emma chose to seek resolve somewhere else—desperately trying to find balance until she drifted away altogether."

Jace stepped forward again, his voice carrying the power of urgency. "If you could confront her, would you? Would you have brought her back? Or would you still let her wander off alone?"

Alex's expression grew tense as he struggled with the weight of Jace's question. "I can't go back, nor would it change the truth of the matter. I do regret not trying harder, but Emma sought shifts within herself that I could not understand."

Suddenly, a sense of urgency flooded through Ruby. "What if I told you she wrote about that urgency in her poetry? About finding the balance between light and darkness?" She leaned closer, her expression sincere.

"Are you serious?" Alex said, his tone shifting as intrigue flickered into his gaze. "She'd never share openly how she felt about those internal struggles—telling betrayal was simply her whisper."

"She did with us. We just read her last poems and her reflections before she vanished. She poured honesty into her art, and it revealed those emotions that needed to be confronted," Ruby said, her heart racing as hope began to blossom. "Join us in unraveling it together. Confront that past —face the pain, then let it reveal the truth."

Alex stood silent, processing Ruby's invitation. The shadows fluttered within him, yet a glimmer of understanding flickered in his eyes.

"I don't know if I'm ready," he admitted at last, the conflict evident in his gaze.

"None of us are," Bella urged gently. "But if we truly care about Emma's memory, we must embrace the shadows rather than run from them. Every step behind the frame might lead us to uncover the entire narrative that still holds weight."

As the weight of their words settled in the air, Ruby felt a rising hope. They were moments away from the ultimate confrontation—not just with Alex, but with the deep-seated fears linked to Emma's journey. The past would reveal its truths, and the light would guide them home.

"Let's take this one step at a time," Jace suggested, his voice as steady as a heartbeat. "We can gather the information, reach out to people who can help connect the dots, and work through this together. Only then will we be ready to face those shadows."

As they began discussing their points of contact, Ruby felt a sense of unity surrounding them. The shadows no longer felt suffocating; instead, they were stepping stones toward understanding Emma. They would face both the light and dark within this twisted narrative, and together they would bring Emma's story back into the light.

With flashlight beams guiding their conversations and revelations igniting hope deep within, they were moving forward—chasing shadows toward the countless truths still waiting to be illuminated.

CHAPTER 24

Ties That Bind

As the weeks turned into a whirlwind of activity, Ruby, Bella, Liv, Jace, and even Alex found themselves at the heart of unraveling Emma's complex narrative. Each day was filled with phone calls, meetings, and discussions that connected them further to Emma's spirit and the people she had left behind. The gathering they organized in the park had blossomed into a community of hope, and the collective testimonials continued to shine light on the shadows of her past.

The day after their confrontation with Alex, the group met at Ruby's apartment to compile everything they had uncovered thus far. The energy in the room crackled with anticipation, layering hope on top of determination.

"Alright, let's map out our next steps," Ruby suggested, her fingers poised over her notebook, ready to connect the dots of their ongoing investigation. "We need to reach out to more people who were present at the gallery that night. We can determine if there are any new leads or connections to Alex we haven't yet considered."

"Agreed! We should also verify the other mentions of Alex over time," Bella added, her excitement bubbling at the potential discoveries. "If he had been a recurring figure in Emma's circle, we need to understand who else was involved."

Liv shuffled through a stack of photographs, her gaze focused intently on the faces of those captured at the park gathering. "Someone could still have information about Emma that ties back to Alex and her last moments. We should also try reaching out to artists she exhibited with. They might remember Emma discussing her feelings about him."

Just as they began sketching an outline of contacts and approaches, the familiar ping of Ruby's phone momentarily distracted her. She eagerly picked it up to glance at the screen, rising excitement coursing through her as she recognized a message from Lila.

"Hey everyone, it's Lila! We want to meet up again this week. Kyle and I found something that might help clarify Emma's relationships and any lingering feelings involving Alex. Can you visit tomorrow in the afternoon?"

The room filled with a palpable surge of energy. "This could change everything!" Ruby exclaimed. "If they found something new, it might be the understanding we need to connect the shadows."

The group spent the evening strategizing, piecing together everything they had gathered and preparing for the meeting with Lila and Kyle. Ruby felt a twinge of excitement mixed with trepidation; what if this new evidence amplified or contradicted what they already knew?

The following day, they arrived at Lila's home, their hearts thumping in unison. Upon stepping inside, they were greeted by the soothing scent of freshly brewed coffee, the warmth of the room washing over them as Lila motioned for them to sit.

"Thank you for coming," she said, her eyes flitting to each of them with visible relief. "Kyle and I spent the night reviewing some of Emma's belongings, and we discovered a few things that could add more depth to our understanding of her emotional state."

Immediately, the energy shifted, filling the room with reverence and anticipation. Ruby couldn't help but draw closer, sensing that the truth they had all longed for was edging closer.

"I found this in her sketchbook," Lila said, revealing a worn notebook filled with Emma's reflections and artwork. "This entry stood out to me."

As she opened the book, Ruby's breath caught in her throat as she read aloud. "Some friendships are anchors that ground you, while others turn into weights that drag you below. I've been drowning in uncertainty... Alex represents the storm, and I fear this storm is going to pull me under."

The room fell silent, the weight of Emma's words hanging in the air, shimmering with both sorrow and clarity. Each phrase painted a vivid picture of Emma's emotional struggle, a haunting reflection of her attempts to navigate the conflicting tides within her life.

"Wow," Liv said softly, her expression serious. "Emma was aware of how her connections affected her—not just with Alex but with all her friendships."

"It definitely adds new dimension to her perspective on relationships," Ruby noted, feeling a swell of empathy for her friend. "But there's more to uncover."

As they continued to thumb through Emma's sketches and journaling, they stumbled upon a folder tucked between the pages. "What's this?" Jace asked, pulling it out carefully.

Inside, they found photocopies of letters—some inked in Emma's handwriting, and others penned by unidentified individuals. The letters contained bits of conversation that Emma had with others, discussing her struggles with emotions and uncertainty, relationships, and her art.

One letter stood out in particular. Ruby read it aloud, her heart racing: "I feel torn between what I want and what has been expected of me. I wonder if the shadows in my life will eventually consume my light, and if anyone will notice when I disappear."

"Did she write this to someone specific?" Bella asked, intrigued.

"It looks like she might have reached out to a mentor from one of her art classes," Ruby noted, glancing through the pages carefully. "This could indicate that she was actively seeking guidance, someone to help her navigate the emotional turmoil."

"That's a vital piece," Kyle chimed in, leaning forward in his seat. "If she was communicating her frustrations and not feeling heard, it reflects a struggle with her identity. Maybe reaching out to this mentor could help us uncover where some of that tension stemmed from."

A surge of adrenaline rushed through the group as they absorbed the weight of their discoveries. This was the deeper emotional landscape they had been searching for—a reflection of how Emma perceived her relationships and herself amid the complexities of life.

"Do we know how to get in touch with this mentor?" Jace asked, holding onto the letters, the excitement raising expectations of what they might discover next.

"Let me check," Lila said, opening the desk drawer. After a moment, she pulled out a business card, turning it toward the group. "This is old, but I believe this might be the information for Emma's mentor, a woman named Clara. She ran several local art workshops."

"If we can locate Clara, she might provide further insight into Emma's emotional struggles leading up to her disappearance," Ruby suggested, feeling a renewed sense of determination coursing through her veins. "Let's contact her as soon as we can."

With fervent intent and new information to guide them, Ruby felt a surge of hope rise in her chest. These layers were aligning in a way that felt significant, making the shadows around Emma's life grow less foreboding.

"We won't stop until we uncover the threads that connect everything," Ruby asserted, her voice steady with conviction as the group rallied around their shared mission, hearts beating in unison.

As the conversation buzzed with excitement about their next steps, Ruby's heart filled with a sense of purpose. They were finally moving toward a breakthrough—a convergence of truths that would not only help them piece together Emma's story but would also reinforce the bonds that connected everyone present.

Each moment, each letter, and every reflection was bringing them closer to unveiling the essence of Emma's life, allowing her light to shine brightly once more. And as the group set their sights on Clara, Ruby sensed they were on the precipice of an important discovery—one that might turn the tide in their quest for the truth.

CHAPTER 25

A New Beginning

As spring seeped into the city and new blooms burst forth in a riot of color, Ruby, Bella, Liv, Jace, and Alex found themselves standing at the edge of a significant turning point. After weeks of gathering testimonies and unearthing Emma's artistic journey, they were finally on the cusp of closure, the end of their journey metamorphosing into the promise of new beginnings.

The group had tracked down Clara, Emma's mentor, and invited her to meet at the same park where they had held the gathering to honor Emma's memory. They hoped she could provide further insights into Emma's emotional state, her connections, and perhaps the critical moments leading to her disappearance.

On a bright Saturday morning, they arranged a makeshift tribute in the park, enhanced by fresh flowers reaping the reward of the season. The sun filtered through the trees, painting dappled patterns on the ground. Each moment felt laden with significance, as if the universe were keenly aware of the importance of their mission.

"I can't thank you all enough for inviting me here," Clara said, stepping forward. Her kind eyes held the wisdom of experiences seldom spoken. She exuded a warmth that guests who attended these gatherings recognized immediately as they embraced the familiar warmth of creative pursuit.

"Thank you for coming, Clara. We're eager to hear anything you can share about Emma," Ruby said, her heart filled with both hope and hesitation. "Your perspective on her journey might hold pivotal clues regarding her emotional struggles."

"I've watched many of my students grow and flourish, but Emma held a special spark," Clara replied, glancing around the park, taking in the vibrant surroundings. "She was passionate, insightful, but also deeply introspective. Her art often reflected a battle between light and shadow—something I sensed she was grappling with on a personal level."

"What do you mean?" Jace asked, intrigued. "Did she share that with you?"

"She confided in me during our one-on-one sessions about her feelings of uncertainty regarding her work and relationships —how they intersected in ways that sometimes felt too heavy for her," Clara explained. "But it was the connections she forged that often inspired her. She felt trapped between her need for acceptance and the fear of losing herself to others' expectations."

"Especially with people like Alex?" Bella probed gently, locking eyes with Clara.

"That's right. Emma was always drawn to those with layers, like Alex, who showed glimpses of darkness. She often reflected on how they affected her sense of self," Clara continued, emotion lacing her words. "There were conversations we had where she wrestled with her feelings, torn between loyalty and the need for personal freedom."

Ruby felt a heat rise in her chest—these were the themes they had been uncovering, woven through Emma's poetry and artwork. "So you think her relationship with Alex stunted her creativity or distorted it?"

"I think their energy created an imbalance," Clara replied. "Their bond brought both inspiration and chaos into her artistic expression. But she never lost her light entirely; she just had to fight for it."

As Clara's words painted glimpses of Emma's spirit, Ruby felt a sense of clarity among the shadows. "Is there a piece of advice you gave her that perhaps resonated?" she asked, hope blooming within her.

"Yes," Clara said, her voice steady and contemplative. "I once told her, 'Art is powerful; it can embrace shadows but still shine brightly. It's the tension that creates depth.' I believe she held on to that idea, even when it felt challenging."

Ruby absorbed the wisdom of Clara's words as they settled into a profoundly intimate moment of remembrance. "Emma sought to embody the conversation between light and darkness in her art. But having both friends and shadows can be just as powerful."

"That's true," Clara said thoughtfully. "But you see, it's also how she learned to confront those shadows. Art was a method of exploration and resolution for Emma. If something felt wrong, she painted through it, all while knowing the core of her vision remained intact."

Tears pricked Ruby's eyes as she felt the magnitude of Emma's spirit swelling within her. "Then let's continue to honor her by allowing her truth to emerge. We can build a narrative reflecting her fight—a narrative alive with vibrancy, renewal, and hope."

As Ruby contemplated their journey, a feeling of synchronicity washed over her. They were no longer just piecing together the fragments; they were actively creating a powerful story that illustrated Emma's life bounded by love and struggling against shadows.

Clara smiled knowingly. "Just remember, Emma's journey isn't tied solely to her struggles. It is also filled with learning, growth, and a passion that extends beyond."

Feeling empowered, Ruby decided that the gathering they hosted in the park would include a section dedicated to Emma's legacy and a chance for attendees to create art in her memory. "We'll channel that spirit into a collaborative mural," she announced, excitement bubbling within her.

"That's a wonderful idea!" Jace said, a grin spreading across his face. "An evolving tribute that embodies what Emma meant for each of us."

As they confirmed plans for the mural, Ruby felt a renewed sense of purpose guiding them forward. They could create an art piece that not only captured Emma's story but also invited others to explore their own narratives, allowing moments of vulnerability and strength to collide beautifully.

As the sun began to dip lower in the sky, the warmth of Emma's spirit enveloped them all. The connection they had forged with Clara and the community echoed with shared understanding, binding them closer as they embraced a collective call to honor Emma's journey.

In the weeks to come, they would work on the mural, interspersing their stories and experiences amidst strokes of color reflecting Emma's essence, incorporating symbols from her art and life. They would chase light through the shadows, ensuring her legacy would flourish.

As Ruby stepped back to take in the joy of the unfolding plans around her, she felt the bonds growing stronger, carrying forth a sense of unity. Emma's spirit swirled among them, reminding Ruby that every time they shone a light, they pulled the mere fragility of existence into a living brilliance.

With each passing day, they committed to uncovering the truth, chasing shadows, and ultimately painting the most beautiful picture — one filled with resolve, love, and a profound connection to the life Emma had led. The new beginning that lay ahead felt overwhelmingly alive, brimming with promise and possibilities, leaving Ruby immersed in the warmth of hope.

CHAPTER 26

The Exhibition

The day of the exhibition arrived, the culmination of weeks of hard work, collaboration, and deep introspection. Ruby, Bella, Liv, Jace, and Alex gathered early in the park, where the collaborative mural had taken shape over the past several days. Each friend had contributed their unique touch, adding vibrant colors and details that mirrored Emma's essence and the stories they had shared together.

As Ruby looked over their creation, her heart swelled with pride and emotion. The mural depicted a magnificent river flowing through colorful landscapes, depicting scenes inspired by Emma's poetry and artwork nestled within lush greenery and sunlight. The element of shadow was omnipresent, yet balanced beautifully by bursts of color and light, reflecting both the struggles and triumphs Emma had faced.

"This is breathtaking," Bella said, stepping back to admire the mural. "I can't believe how much each of us poured our hearts into this!"

"It's truly a testament to Emma's spirit," Ruby added, beaming at her friends. "This can serve as a reminder that even amidst the shadows, we all can find a place to shine."

As they put the final touches on the display, attendees started to gather, drawn by the vibrant artwork. Families, friends, and community members filled the park, their eyes widening in appreciation as they took in the mural. Ruby could see familiar faces mixing with new ones, all here to celebrate Emma's artistry and spirit.

"Are we ready to open?" Jace asked, adjusting the small placard that announced the exhibition.

"Definitely," Ruby replied. "I can't wait to share her story with everyone."

A hush fell over the crowd as Ruby stepped in front of the gathering, the weight of the moment enveloping her. She took a deep breath, feeling Emma's spirit guiding her. "Thank you all for coming today to honor Emma's memory," she began, her voice steady but filled with emotion. "Art should capture not only the beauty of life but also the depths of our struggles; it's a bridge connecting each of us in this community. Over the past several weeks, we've worked together to create this mural."

She gestured to the painting, the collective spirit of the group blending seamlessly with their dedication. "Each brushstroke embodies Emma's journey—a reminder that light exists despite the shadows we often face."

As she spoke, Ruby could see nods of understanding ripple through the crowd; her words resonated with a shared history, capturing the essence of Emma's impact on their lives.

"With this exhibition, we hope to bring forward Emma's truth and remind everyone of the power that resides within us all — to shine in our own uniqueness amid the complexities of life."

The crowd erupted into applause, and Ruby felt warmth spread within her as she locked eyes with her friends, their shared resolve igniting a fire of hope that filled the air.

After the speech, attendees dispersed to explore the mural, each becoming enveloped in the emotions that swirled around them. Ruby watched as they shared anecdotes, laughter, and whispers of admiration, creating a tapestry of recollections as they reminisced together.

As the day wore on, Ruby noticed Alex lingering at the edge of the crowd, watching the proceedings with an intensity that made the shadows in his eyes deeper. She walked over to him, sensing his vulnerability.

"Alex, what do you think?" Ruby asked, her voice gentle, hoping to draw him out of himself during this moment of healing.

"It's beautiful," he said honestly, his eyes glistening as he took in the mural. "Emma would've loved to see this. You all captured her spirit more thoroughly than I ever did."

"Didn't we all share in the spirit of her journey?" Ruby replied, her heart softened by his sincerity. "This place is a reminder that she's still here, even in absence. Each story shared adds new layers to her legacy."

"That's what frightens me," he admitted, the weight of his emotions surfacing. "In trying to capture her essence, we're also confronting the reality of what I lost. I'm still breaking that connection to the shadows I lived in. Seeing all these portraits and reflections illuminates the past I've hidden from."

"Shadows can be daunting, but they also reveal depth," Ruby encouraged gently. "By stepping into this space, you're allowing your light to chase away the darkness you've felt. You participated with us to honor her—so let that be part of your journey as well."

At that moment, Alex nodded, a glimmer of understanding flickering in his gaze. "I've been avoiding my emotions, clinging to the shadows. But I want to confront the past, pay homage to Emma — face my connection with her and move on."

Feeling a surge of hope, Ruby turned to a nearby group just as a cheerful laughter broke through the crowd. "This feels like a community rebirth," she said, her heart swelling. "Emma's legacy has ignited something beautiful among us."

As the sun began its descent, casting a warm glow over the park, Ruby felt exhilaration and anticipation thrive within her.

Just then, a family approached the exhibit — Emma's parents, Lila and Kyle, stepping forward with uncertain but hopeful expressions. They had arrived late but in time to witness the unveiling of their daughter's spirit.

"Thank you for doing this; it means more than you can imagine," Lila said, tears glistening in her eyes as she took in the mural.

"Emma would've been proud," Kyle added, his voice low but filled with gratitude.

Ruby's heart constricted at the sight of them standing before the artwork—this was the moment she had been yearning for: the shared bond between those who loved Emma, now woven together by the artistry they had collectively honored.

With newfound purpose, Ruby spoke to them directly. "We wanted to make sure Emma's legacy lived on through everyone who knew her. Sharing her story through this mural connects us all; it's about vulnerability, strength, and love."

Lila reached out, her trembling hand brushing against the mural's surface, whispering softly, "I can feel her here."

"I hope we've captured the depth of her journey," Ruby said with sincerity. "There's power in bringing these memories forward, and we could never have done it without the support of all of you."

The crowd gathered around them, sharing in achingly beautiful moments of reminiscence. Conversations unfolded seamlessly, echoes of shared experiences filling the air. As they shared memories, Ruby stood immersed in gratitude, the connection flowing between each person like a radiant thread woven through the tapestry spread before them.

The sun cast long shadows, merging light with darkness as the day began to wind down. Ruby glanced at Alex, watching him slowly engage in conversation with other attendees. She felt a sense of peace flow through her; the transformation was beginning. Emma's spirit joined them, weaving itself among the attendees, infusing each moment with a sense of hope.

As the evening progressed, Ruby and her friends invited everyone to share their pieces of Emma's life — their art, memories, and reflections coalescing into a community of healing. The mural had transformed into a canvas that not only embodied Emma's creativity but also became a vessel for the emotions they all held for her.

By the time the stars began to appear, Ruby felt an overwhelming surge of love surround them. It was not only a tribute to Emma's artistry but also an affirmation of their journey — confronting their fears, discovering the light that resided within shadows, and embracing the ties that bound them all together.

In that moment, Ruby realized they had turned a corner; they had created a safe space for vulnerability to flourish, a sanctuary where memories wove seamlessly into newfound hope.

As they lit candles in honor of Emma, Ruby closed her eyes, feeling the warmth of the flames flickering in the night air, a symbol of her light. Each candle brought forth the connections they had built, allowing Emma's spirit to shine brighter than it ever could in the shadows.

"Together, we'll continue to honor her," Ruby whispered, feeling the warmth of her friends beside her as they reflected on the evening. "This is just the beginning."

As the gathered community stepped forward, revealing their memories and emotions, Ruby felt a wave of exhilaration propel them into their next chapter. They were no longer just chasing shadows—they had stepped into the light and embraced the connections that would forever tie them to Emma's spirit and the legacy that would echo, undeterred, through time.

CHAPTER 27

Unexpected Visitors

The aftermath of the exhibition had indelibly marked a turning point for Ruby, Bella, Liv, Jace, and Alex. The vibrant tribute to Emma transformed the park into a sanctuary of memories and solidarity, solidifying connections among friends and new acquaintances alike. Word of the exhibit spread through the community like wildfire, igniting conversations around Emma's legacy and the importance of keeping her spirit alive.

In the days that followed, Ruby found solace in the routine of their investigation. They continued to reach out to Emma's family, friends, and colleagues, meticulously piecing together the fragments of her story. Each new connection brought insights, sometimes painful but always poignant. They were no longer merely chasing shadows; they were unveiling intricate narratives that demanded to be heard.

One crisp afternoon, Ruby sat at her kitchen table reviewing notes and sketches. A warm cup of tea sat steaming next to her, providing comfort amid her notes on Emma's life. As she wrote down her thoughts, Bella and Liv joined her, animatedly discussing future plans for more installations to celebrate Emma's artistry.

"What do you think about setting up a art walk?" Bella suggested, her excitement palpable. "We could include local artists to inspire ongoing creativity in the community. It could keep Emma's legacy thriving!"

"Definitely! We could invite those who knew her and gather stories as people walk through the art," Liv added. "It'd create an open dialogue that honors her impact."

Before Ruby could respond, a sudden knock at the door interrupted their discussion. It was a solid rap, urgent and unexpected. A flicker of confusion shot through Ruby as she exchanged glances with her friends.

"Who could that be?" Liv asked, brow furrowing.

"Let's check it out," Ruby replied, rising from her seat, her heart racing as uncertainty flickered in her mind. She approached the door, slowly opening it to find two figures standing on her doorstep: it was Lila and Kyle, Emma's parents, faces filled with concern and urgency.

"Ruby!" Lila exclaimed, her voice tight with urgency. "We need to talk. Something has come up."

"Please, come in!" Ruby stepped back, allowing Lila and Kyle to enter. "What's wrong?"

"We didn't expect to see you again so soon," Kyle said, running a hand nervously through his hair. "We're sorry for showing up unannounced, but there's something important you need to hear."

Ruby exchanged worried glances with her friends, the tension in the room thickening. "What's happened?"

Lila took a deep breath before speaking, visibly shaken. "We received a strange message last night. Someone claiming to know about Emma reached out to us—someone who insisted on meeting."

"A witness?" Jace asked, stepping forward, intrigued yet cautious.

"Yes, and they claimed to have seen her near the river shortly before she disappeared," Lila explained. "But they wanted to remain anonymous and insisted that we didn't involve the authorities."

"Why wouldn't they want us to contact the police?" Bella questioned, her voice laced with concern. "If this person holds vital information, they should come forward."

"They mentioned they were afraid of retribution—afraid of something lurking in the shadows. They specifically referenced 'being silenced' if we contacted the police," Kyle replied, his face pale. "It sounded ominous."

Ruby felt a chill race down her spine, the implications of the warning settling heavily. "What do you think we should do?"

"We need to meet them—hear what they have to say," Lila declared. "But we should approach this cautiously. It feels like the balance between light and darkness is tipping, and we can't afford to lose anyone else in this struggle."

"What are the details of the meeting?" Liv asked, her brow furrowed.

Lila rifled through her bag and pulled out a scrap of paper. "The person said to meet at the very spot Emma used to sit and sketch by the river. They want to do this away from prying eyes."

The location brought a wave of unease, reminding Ruby of Emma's final moments — the shadows that encircled her spirit just before she vanished. "When is the meeting?"

"Tomorrow evening," Kyle confirmed, glancing anxiously at Ruby. "We thought it best to come to you first before making any rash decisions. We trust you."

"Then let's proceed carefully," Ruby said decisively. "We'll go together. The four of us can back you up if things feel off. We aren't letting any shadows cloud this potential lead."

"Thank you," Lila whispered, her voice trembling with gratitude. "We couldn't do this without you."

With the plans set for their meeting looming over the next day, Ruby's mind swirled with thoughts and fears. But beneath the unease lay a flicker of determination. Their journey had been steeped in shadows, but with every twist and turn, they had drawn closer to uncovering Emma's legacy.

The next evening, tension mounted as the sun began to dip below the horizon, casting a blanket of twilight over the city. The group assembled at Ruby's apartment, adrenaline coursing through their veins as they gathered for the meeting.

"Are you all ready?" Ruby asked, her voice steadying her own nerves as she glanced at her friends. The determination reflected in their eyes soothed her worries, and they nodded in affirmation.

"Let's stick together and stay focused," Jace reminded, echoing the sentiment they had all felt since beginning this journey.

As they walked to the riverbank, the evening air felt charged with uncertainty, the shadows lengthening as the sun dipped lower. Ruby could feel the tension in the atmosphere, an electric current that swelled with possibility and fear. Every step felt like it echoed in the silence, amplifying the weight of the moment.

When they arrived at the spot where Emma had often sketched, the world fell still. The river shimmered under the soft glow of the moonlight, casting shimmering reflections that danced on the water's surface. And there, standing a few feet down the bank, was a figure cloaked in darkness, watching them closely.

"Is that them?" Liv whispered, her voice barely above the gentle rustle of leaves in the breeze.

"I guess we'll find out," Ruby replied, her heart pounding as she stepped forward cautiously.

As they approached, the figure turned to face them, revealing a young man with dark hair and a pensive expression etched onto his face. "You came," he stated, his voice a mixture of relief and apprehension.

"You said you had information about Emma?" Ruby prompted, feeling the weight of the moment settle upon her.

"Yes," he replied slowly, glancing nervously toward the water, as if afraid of being overheard. "I'm not here to involve anyone else, but I saw her that night. I was lingering near the river when she was there, speaking with a guy who looked upset."

Ruby felt a surge of urgency. "Was it Alex?"

He nodded hesitantly. "Yes, but they seemed to be arguing about more than who was with whom. They were both blocked by shadows cast by the bridge, and I could see the fear in Emma's eyes."

"What happened next?" Jace asked, urgency rising in his voice.

"The argument escalated. Emma turned to leave, and Alex... he reached for her. I heard her shout, pleading, but she never came back." The young man's voice broke, emotions tightening around his chest.

"I wanted to intervene, but fear held me back. When Emma called out, it felt like a moment crushed by the weight of whatever darkness encumbered both of them," he continued, visibly shaken.

"That means something did go awry after the argument," Ruby said sharply, each word solidifying the pieces of their investigation in her mind. "Did you see where Emma went afterward?"

The young man hesitated, pain flaring in his eyes. "I lost sight of her. I wanted to call for help, but the tension in the air stilled me. When I finally worked up the courage to reach out, I scanned the area but saw nothing."

The revelation felt like a lead weight anchoring in Ruby's heart, the shadows chasing Emma away in that fleeting moment magnifying the eternal loss. "You did the right thing by coming forward with this," she said gently, trying to fill the silence with compassion.

Before the young man could respond, the sound of footsteps echoed from behind them, drawing Ruby's attention. Her breath caught as she turned to see Alex striding toward them, expression wild and imploring.

"Stop!" he shouted, his voice filled with urgency. "You don't want to be involved with him! You don't know what you're getting into!"

"The witnesses are important, Alex," Ruby pressed back, her determination unyielding. "What happened that night is crucial for understanding what happened to Emma!"

"Get out of this while you can!" Alex warned, stepping forward, shadows thickening around him.

Ruby felt a flicker of vulnerability resurface, but she steeled herself. "You need to acknowledge the truth — about what went down that night and how it might have triggered consequences beyond just words exchanged."

"What do you want from me?" Alex replied, desperation creeping into his voice. "I told you I was in the dark, and nothing about that night benefited anyone—neither Emma nor I!"

The tension peaked, and the group fell silent, feeling the weight of conflict settle billowing around like a storm. For a moment, it felt as if time hung suspended in the air, ready to tear apart as emotions clashed against one another.

"I want the truth, Alex," Ruby cried, her eyes turning fierce. "It's time to confront the shadows. Each moment we waste pushes Emma's legacy further into the abyss."

The young man who had witnessed the confrontation watched the exchange intently, his gaze flitting between Ruby and Alex.

Finally, Alex's shoulders sagged, the tumult of emotions flickering across his face. "I didn't know…" He finally answered, conviction settling in as shadows blended with light around him. "But now I see! Emma was searching for understanding—a path away from the storms we created."

Behind Alex's candor, a new possibility emerged—a shared vulnerability that might lead them to insights they needed.

"I'm here to seek anonymity, not replace the light," the young witness spoke quietly, conviction rising amidst the tension. "But if you're willing to confront how everything unspooled, maybe we can chase these shadows together."

Ruby felt the shift in the air as the resolve tightened among them. The shadows that had haunted Emma during her final days wove into the fabric of their stories, carving paths toward revelation. They were set on unveiling the untold truths that echoed amidst their fears.

"Together," Ruby said, her voice steady and filled with conviction. "We can bring Emma's legacy back into the light."

In that moment, amidst the swirling ghosts of unspoken truth and confrontation with their past, they understood: only by collaborating could they navigate the labyrinthine shadows, reclaim the narrative that had been lost, and light the way toward healing.

As the sky darkened further, shadows retreated in the presence of the flickering friendships bound together, igniting a fire of hope, courage, and renewed strength. The confrontation had taken place, and now the group could dive deeper into the truths waiting just beyond the frame, guiding them toward a future that could still embrace Emma's vibrant essence.

CHAPTER 28

Reflection

The sun hung low in the sky, casting long shadows across the park where Ruby, Bella, Liv, Jace, and Alex had gathered once more. It had been a month since the exhibition dedicated to Emma, and the vibrant mural created in her honor remained a testament to her spirit. The park, once a backdrop for uncertainty, now radiated a warmth, with whispers of Emma's laughter echoing in the gentle breeze.

As they settled on a bench near the mural, Ruby could feel a palpable shift among them—one of reflection and gratitude as they prepared to reflect on their journey. Each person had undergone a transformation, a cathartic release, and the evocation of shared memories cultivated the spirit of community they had fostered together.

"I can't believe how much has happened in such a short time," Liv began, looking across the mural's brilliant colors that danced in the sunlight. "It's surreal to think we've unveiled so many layers of Emma's life—and our own in the process."

"It feels like we've not only remembered her but also rediscovered parts of ourselves through this journey," Bella added thoughtfully, her eyes scanning the mural, her heart visibly swelling. "We each came together because of Emma, but what we've built transcends that connection."

Jace nodded in agreement. "Digging deep into Emma's art and the stories surrounding her life has revealed so much about who we are. We were chasing shadows, but we ended up capturing so much light. It feels like we liberated a narrative that desperately needed to be told."

"I think it's incredible how art connects us," Ruby interjected, her heart brimming with affection for her friends. "Even during our darkest moments, Emma's pieces reminded us that behind every shadow, bright colors can emerge. Her artistic voice reunited all of us and bridged gaps we may not have known existed."

Alex listened intently, contemplating the words shared among them. "I spent so long in darkness, fighting my own demons and ignoring the significance of the relationships that mattered. But through this journey to uncover Emma's story, I've realized the weight of responsibility I carried. This process has opened my eyes, and for the first time in a long while, I see the power of connection."

Ruby turned to Alex, a gentle smile spreading across her lips. "You've shown courage by facing your past and pursuing the truth. Honoring Emma needed her spirit to shine through you as well. We're all here for each other."

Before long, the conversation drifted into a reflective discussion about shifting perspectives and newfound friendships. The threads of their collective journey were beginning to weave a fabric of healing that transcended the tragedy of Emma's disappearance.

"Looking back, I realize how fear clouded my judgment," Alex said slowly, his voice tinged with vulnerability. "I didn't want to acknowledge how important Emma was to me, nor did I manage my own struggles properly. I've learned now how crucial it is to face our feelings before they spiral downward."

Liv reached out for Alex's hand, an act that bridged the gap between them, encapsulating the essence of understanding they had built together. "That's the beauty of transformation. It allows us to grow and find new ways to engage with those we care about. Emma's story helped us recognize that change is possible."

As the group remained united under the glowing sun, Ruby felt the urge to acknowledge the profound journey they had undertaken. "Perhaps we should create something new—a collaborative piece that embodies everything we've experienced together through Emma's story."

"What do you have in mind?" Bella asked, intrigue dancing in her eyes.

"I'm thinking we could compile the stories shared during the exhibition, art inspired by Emma, and the essence of our collective reflections," Ruby proposed, her imagination igniting with possibilities. "We could turn this journey into a book—a narrative that intertwines her legacy with our connections, our experiences. It would be a tribute that represents rebirth and growth."

"Yes! That would seamlessly combine art and storytelling," Liv exclaimed, her excitement palpable. "We could showcase Emma's work alongside pieces created by each of us, intertwined with our reflections on her journey."

The idea electrified the air among them. Ruby felt a sense of purpose solidifying, the flicker of camaraderie igniting into a steady flame. "We owe it to ourselves and to Emma to preserve this moment in art and story," Ruby concluded, fueled by the burgeoning enthusiasm within her friends.

With a shared commitment to the task at hand, the group began brainstorming ideas, drawing on their emotions, experiences, and memories of Emma. They envisioned a beautiful mosaic of narratives—each chapter intertwining poignant moments, sketches, and testimonies that paid tribute to the vibrant woman who had brought them all together.

As the sun dipped on the horizon, casting hues of pink and purple across the sky, Ruby closed her eyes and felt the gentle breeze wrap around her. In that peaceful moment, she breathed deeply, embracing the culmination of their efforts and the new beginning blossoming before them.

"Let's make this happen," she declared as her friends nodded enthusiastically. "Together, we can transform our collective journey into something meaningful. It won't just honor Emma; it will celebrate the paths we walked in unison."

At that moment, with the sun setting behind them and shadows dancing along the ground, Ruby realized this was not just about Emma—it was about them. The trust and bonds that had formed amidst the chaos had given rise to a new beginning, one that promised to chase away darkness and bring forth understanding through connection and expression.

As sunlight faded into twilight, they stood together, a tapestry of diverse colors and narratives woven intricately by their experiences, a promise blooming for the future—a shared legacy of love, art, and transformation that would keep Emma's spirit glowing brightly in the hearts of all who remembered.

CHAPTER 29

Emerging Light

The day of the book launch finally arrived, and Ruby could hardly contain her excitement. After weeks of diligent work, collaborations, and introspection, they had compiled a beautiful collection of Emma's artwork, writings, and their narratives into a book titled Emerging Light: The Legacy of Emma Lane. Each page captured not only Emma's vibrant spirit but also the connections forged through the shared journey of uncovering her life and legacy.

As Ruby stepped into the community center where the launch was set to take place, she felt her pulse race with anticipation. The hall was bright and inviting, adorned with flowers and art that echoed Emma's colorful essence. The mural they had painted together stood proudly on display, serving as a centerpiece for the occasion, bearing witness to the beauty of collaboration and the power of art to heal and unite.

"Wow, Ruby, this looks incredible!" Bella exclaimed as she twirled around, admiring the decorations they had set up. "You really brought everything together beautifully."

"Thank you!" Ruby responded, her heart swelling with gratitude and pride. "I couldn't have done it without all of you. This is truly a collective effort."

Liv set out copies of the book on a table near the mural, each cover bedecked with a print of one of Emma's mesmerizing paintings. "I can't believe how far we've come," Liv said, glancing around in awe. "It feels surreal to be here."

"All those late nights and moments of anxiety turned into this — an opportunity to honor Emma and share her story with everyone," Jace added, adjusting his glasses as he stacked the books neatly.

As attendees began to arrive, Ruby turned to see Lila and Kyle entering the hall. Immediately, she felt a rush of emotion watching Emma's parents step in, their faces reflecting mixed feelings of anticipation and nostalgia. They had both been so supportive throughout this journey, and it was evident how significant this moment was for them.

"Hello again!" Lila greeted warmly, her eyes scanning the beautifully arranged tables and decorations. "This is wonderful, Ruby. It really captures Emma's essence!"

"Thank you for being a part of this. We wanted to create a space where everyone can celebrate her legacy," Ruby replied, fighting back tears of happiness.

As the hall filled with friends, family, and community members, Ruby felt the atmosphere buzz with excitement and chatter. Old acquaintances reunited, exchanging stories about Emma and their cherished memories. Laughter mingled with a sense of reverence, building an atmosphere reminiscent of hope and healing.

When the time came for Ruby to speak, she felt a mix of excitement and trepidation. Standing at the front of the hall, her heart raced as she glanced around. "I want to thank everyone for coming here today," she began, her voice steadying amid the sea of familiar faces. "We gather to honor Emma and her remarkable legacy, to acknowledge the impact she had on our lives, and to embrace the connections that brought us all together."

Cheers and applause erupted from the crowd, energizing Ruby even further. "This book we've created is a testament to her spirit and our shared journey. It represents more than just stories; it embodies the connections we formed through laughter, joy, pain, and understanding. Emma's light lives on in each page, reminding us that love and hope can emerge even in the darkest of times."

As she spoke, Ruby couldn't help but notice how the warmth radiated through the crowd. Emma's family beamed with pride, embodying the love that resonated for their daughter — their presence a living reminder of the legacy they were celebrating.

"Now, I invite you all to share your own stories," Ruby continued, her excitement bubbling over as she glanced at the faces in the crowd. "This is a gathering for reflections, where we can honor Emma's memory together."

One by one, individuals stepped forward, pouring their hearts out, recounting their cherished memories with Emma. As stories unfolded, Ruby felt tears welling in her eyes. The love and admiration shared transformed the room into a sanctuary, weaving a tapestry of narratives interconnected by Emma's spirit.

Someone recalled how Emma had devoted time to teach a child in the community how to draw, while others chimed in, sharing humorous anecdotes about the lengths Emma would go to help those in need. Each voice defended how they wouldn't be who they were without her influence.

As the emotional atmosphere swelled, Lila stepped forward, her voice trembling with gratitude and pride. "Emma always had this way of making everyone feel valued," she began. "Thank you for celebrating her, for keeping her memory alive."

After several poignant remarks, Alex surprised everyone by stepping forward, a hesitant expression layered with vulnerability on his face. "I want to say something, too," he stated, shifting nervously. "I didn't understand the impact Emma had on my life until I began to confront my own shadows. She showed me how art can illuminate the complexities of love and sorrow."

His admission hung in the air for a moment. "I see now that my fears drove a wedge between us. I am deeply sorry for the pain I caused. I've spent so long in the dark. For that, my apologies to her and all of you who loved her."

The crowd fell silent, absorbing his honesty. Given who and where he stood, Ruby felt an overwhelming sense of forgiveness and unity wash over her. The shadows were lifting—the light embracing even those who had once carried darker burdens.

As the event progressed, Ruby and her friends navigated conversations with attendees, accepting hugs and heartfelt sentiments in memory of Emma. At one point, someone brought forth photographs that had previously gone unseen, illuminating forgotten moments that still shimmered with joy.

With laughter mingling with nostalgia and tears, Ruby felt the circle of remembrance wrapping tightly around her heart. Each story unveiled another layer of Emma's character, painting her presence with more warmth than sorrow.

After hours of celebration, the sun began to set, casting a warm glow through the large windows of the community center. The atmosphere felt vibrant, filled with camaraderie and connection as people began to depart.

As they helped pack away the remaining books and materials, Ruby felt an undeniable shift within her. The experience had woven bonds that extended beyond grief, a community restored and tied together by their shared love for Emma.

"Can you believe how beautifully this turned out?" Liv said, her heart radiating joy. "The connections tonight were powerful!"

"I think we truly captured Emma, and in doing so, we've also begun to embrace our essays and chapters. We've merged our experiences into something real and lasting," Bella added, grinning.

Ruby nodded, her heart swelling with gratitude. "And this is just the beginning. Moving forward, this Emerging Light project can grow, inspiring even more art and creativity within our community."

"Let's create workshop events, mentorship programs—anything that continues the legacy Emma left," Jace said, the passion in his voice igniting new energy among them.

As they left the community center, the warmth of connection enveloped them, and Ruby felt Emma's spirit illuminating their paths. They had turned a chapter filled with struggle into one of hope, unity, and newfound creativity.

The shadows had not only receded; they had revealed a radiant light that now guided them. Each day ahead held the chance to explore the intricacies of life inspired by Emma's art, and as Ruby took a deep breath, she knew without a doubt that they had stepped into a new beginning—one that would honor their friend in all the ways she deserved.

CHAPTER 30

Moving Forward

In the months that followed the exhibition and the outpouring of love for Emma, Ruby, Bella, Liv, Jace, and Alex transformed their grief into action. The launch of Emerging Light: The Legacy of Emma Lane had ignited a passionate movement in their community. Inspired by Emma's spirit, they organized monthly art workshops, open mic nights, and community gatherings centered around creativity and expression—each event aimed at celebrating the intersection of light and shadow in their lives.

The atmosphere in Ruby's apartment felt distinctly different now, infused with a sense of purpose and warmth. Laughter echoed off the walls, mingling with the sound of music playing softly in the background as Ruby prepared for the latest gathering.

"Can you believe it's been six months?" Liv mused, rummaging through a box of supplies labeled "Art Night." "It feels like just yesterday we were scrambling to put together the exhibit."

"I know! Time flies when you're busy creating and honoring Emma," Bella replied, setting up snacks on the table. "It's become such a bright spot in our community. I still feel her energy every time we gather."

Ruby smiled, her heart swelling with a mix of nostalgia and joy. "It really has changed everything. We're turning our pain into something beautiful, and it feels right."

Jace flipped through a collage book filled with photos from their events, from laughter-filled workshops to inspiring performances. "These memories truly highlight how we've connected with others and shared our passion for art collectively. It's amazing to see how our community is thriving."

A knock at the door interrupted their conversation as Ruby went to answer it. Standing before her were familiar faces — Lila and Kyle, Emma's parents. They stood with buoyant smiles, each holding a bouquet of wildflowers that mirrored the vibrant spirit of the artwork they had celebrated together.

"We wanted to surprise you all," Lila said, her eyes shining. "This is our way of saying thank you for everything you've done for Emma. It's been heartwarming to see her memory come alive again."

"Thank you for being a part of this journey," Kyle added, stepping inside, the love radiating from their presence. "What you're doing is so important and fills a void we thought could never be healed."

Ruby glanced at her friends, her heart swelling with gratitude. "I can't express how much that means to us. We've all come together to make something beautiful from the shadows."

After the initial excitement settled, they all sat around the table, the conversation blending seamlessly into familiar topics — stories of their experiences since the exhibition, personal growth, and the connections formed within the community.

"I've been working on my own artistic pieces since we organized the workshops," Lila shared proudly. "I never thought I'd pick up a brush again, but reflecting on Emma's legacy has rekindled my creative spirit."

"That's incredible!" Bella said, her voice filled with encouragement. "You should share your work at one of our upcoming events. Everyone would love to see your pieces."

Lila's face brightened at the idea, an emotional glimmer lighting her eyes. "I would love that. Emma always believed art is most powerful when shared—universal truths found in individual expressions."

Ruby felt a rush of warmth in her chest. "This is what we hoped for—creating a space for everyone to explore their creativity, a testament to the impact Emma had on our lives, and what her spirit continues to inspire."

As the small gathering drew to a close, Ruby felt a shift of purpose wash over her again, strengthening her resolve to keep moving forward. They weren't merely reminiscing about Emma; they were nurturing a blossoming legacy that would continue past the confines of grief.

"Let's open up a dialogue within the community about mental health and support," Jace suggested as they cleansed the remnants of the gathering from the table. "Many of us face our own shadows, and this space we create can aid in cultivating that dialogue."

"I agree," Ruby replied thoughtfully. "Recognizing our shadows while celebrating our light can lead us to deeper connections where healing and creativity flourish."

The friends shared their plans, excited by the possibilities that lay ahead. Ruby glanced out the window at the cityscape, the sun setting over the horizon, painting the sky in brilliant shades of orange and indigo. The world outside seemed imbued with new energy and promise.

In the coming weeks, Ruby and her friends worked diligently to organize more events that allowed space for creativity, vulnerability, and open conversations within the community. They invited speakers to discuss mental health and coping mechanisms, encouraging individuals to peer into their own shadows while supporting one another in their journeys. Each event deepened the bonds they had forged and created new connections to people far and wide, uniting them all in their love for Emma.

As Ruby stood at the forefront of each gathering, welcoming attendees and sharing stories, she felt Emma's spirit wrapping around her like a warm embrace. She was sharing not only her memory but also striking the chords of connection that passed from person to person. Emma's light danced through the space, brightening paths that had once felt dark and lonely.

One evening, during a particularly successful art night, Ruby paused, taking in the vibrant scene around her. Artists were displaying their work, musicians were tuning their instruments, and laughter bubbled over from every corner of the room. Emma's memory lingered like an echo, reminding them that beauty and courage reside in the delicate balance between shadows and light.

"Are you alright?" Liv asked, noticing Ruby's contemplative silence.

"Yes," Ruby replied, her heart swelling. "I just realized how far we've come. It's more than just about remembering Emma; it's about how we've learned to embrace the light each of us carries. We're fostering a community that recognizes the importance of connection and storytelling."

As the event came to a close, Ruby felt a lingering sense of resolve wrap around her, binding everyone present, as if the audience shared one beating heart. With expressions of gratitude filling the room, it was clear they were more than just a group of individuals—they had become an extended family, united by love, healing, and remembrance.

And so, as the evening wound down and the city bathed in the soft embrace of night, Ruby understood that they had forged a new beginning together—one that would honor Emma's legacy, embrace the tethers of life that bind them, and help them navigate the shadows that lingered in the corners of their hearts.

Hand in hand, they stepped forward together, ready for whatever new adventures lay ahead, united against the shadows of the past and illuminated by the light of memories that would always shine through.